D0517520

BONE
DEEP

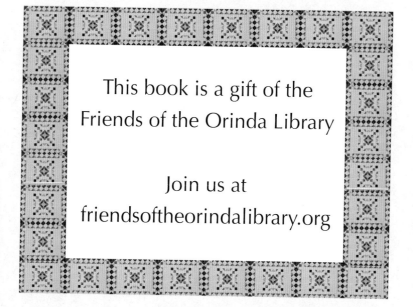

This book is a gift of the
Friends of the Orinda Library

Join us at
friendsoftheorindalibrary.org

Other books in the
Peggy Henderson Adventure series

Reading the Bones
Broken Bones

Also by Gina McMurchy-Barber

Free as a Bird

A Peggy Henderson Adventure

BONE DEEP

Gina McMurchy-Barber

DUNDURN
TORONTO

Editor: Carrie Gleason
Design: Jennifer Gallinger
Cover design by Carmen Giraudy
Author photo by Sandi Wallin

Cover images: Green Girl © Nada Juriši´c
Shipwreck: © Marinicev/iStock
Anchor: © Stephen Coburn/
Shutterstock
Printer: Webcom

Library and Archives Canada Cataloguing in Publication

McMurchy-Barber, Gina, author
        Bone deep / Gina McMurchy-Barber.

(A Peggy Henderson adventure)
Issued in print and electronic formats.
ISBN 978-1-4597-1401-4 (pbk.).--ISBN 978-1-4597-1402-1 (pdf).--
ISBN 978-1-4597-1403-8 (epub)

        I. Title. II. Series: McMurchy-Barber, Gina. Peggy
Henderson adventure.

PS8625.M86B65 2014   jC813'.6   C2014-901021-4   C2014-901022-2

1   2   3   4   5   18   17   16   15   14

ONTARIO ARTS COUNCIL
CONSEIL DES ARTS DE L'ONTARIO
an Ontario government agency
un organisme du gouvernement de l'Ontario

Conseil des Arts du Canada   Canada Council for the Arts   Canada

We acknowledge the support of the **Canada Council for the Arts** and the **Ontario Arts Council** for our publishing program. We also acknowledge the financial support of the **Government of Canada** through the **Canada Book Fund** and **Livres Canada Books**, and the **Government of Ontario** through the **Ontario Book Publishing Tax Credit** and the **Ontario Media Development Corporation**.

Care has been taken to trace the ownership of copyright material used in this book. The author and the publisher welcome any information enabling them to rectify any references or credits in subsequent editions.

J. Kirk Howard, President

The publisher is not responsible for websites or their content unless they are owned by the publisher.

Printed and bound in Canada.

Visit us at
*Dundurn.com | @dundurnpress | Facebook.com/dundurnpress |
Pinterest.com/dundurnpress*

Dundurn
3 Church Street, Suite 500
Toronto, Ontario, Canada
M5E 1M2

Dedicated to Dave, my best friend

ACKNOWLEDGEMENTS

I would like to thank my editor, Carrie Gleason, for her good questions and careful editing of my manuscript. I would also like to thank Aileen Hunter for introducing me to the work of John R. Jewitt, whose shipwreck experiences inspired aspects of my story.

PROLOGUE

June 25th, 1812

In our hasty departure from Tlatskwala Island the Intrepid *struck an outcrop of submerged rocks that tore open her hull. We are taking on water to the measure of two feet an hour and there is little time left for us.*

In this, my final entry as captain, I accept full responsibility for our present calamity. We were trading with natives who call themselves Kwakwaka'wakw at the northern tip of Vancouver's Island. Upon our arrival I sensed an uneasiness previously not experienced in our dealings with the Northwest Indians. In no time relations soured when their sensibilities became disturbed over a difference of opinion during trade negotiations. Chief Noomki was insulted and his warriors retaliated by ambushing our ship in the night. Though my men were caught off guard, they fought admirably and eventually regained control of the ship. Many are now wounded and, tragically, our sailmaker, Thomas Williams, and Mister Astor's trading partner, Robert Lockhart, are dead.

To avoid further attack, I ordered we pull up anchor and set sail. This decision proved to be fatal when, soon after, a tempestuous squall rose up, interfering with our visibility and control over the ship. It was exactly 3 o'clock when we struck the unseen obstacle hidden below the surface of the water.

Intrepid *is fitted with two dories, hardly sufficient for the entire crew. Upon my orders they are preparing to abandon ship. They are taking what they can in way of food rations. As captain I will stay at my post and oversee the evacuation of the crew or until the ship goes down, whichever comes first. I placed the responsibility for leading the men to safety onto my first mate, Mister Carver. He will deliver this journal into the hands of my employer, should he be so fortunate to make it back to New York alive.*

I painfully regret that I failed in my duties and as a result Intrepid *and her cargo are lost. I pray the Lord has mercy on my men and sees them safely home.*

"Take me up, and cast me forth into the sea; so shall the sea be calm unto you." Jonah 1:12

Captain James Whittaker

CHAPTER ONE

It was Sunday afternoon and everyone in the house was in a stink — the floors had to be scrubbed, the curtains vacuumed, dozens of knickknacks dusted — all because Great Aunt Beatrix was coming to visit. There couldn't have been more fuss made had she been the Queen of England coming for her Diamond Jubilee. On top of having to give up a perfectly good Sunday in early June to clean house, I was expected to vacate my bedroom too.

"My room! Why does Aunt Beatrix get my room?" I blurted when I first got the news. "Where am I supposed to read, or do homework, or eat in peace?"

"Oh Peggy," Mom snorted. "You sound like Eeyore." I hated it when she compared me to characters in *Winnie-the-Pooh*.... When was she ever going to remember I wasn't a little kid? "Besides, you know Aunt Margaret doesn't like it when you eat in your room." Mom was changing the subject, but I wasn't going to let her get away with it.

"I still don't get why I have to be the one to sleep on the sofa. She's your aunt — why don't you give up your room, or for that matter why not Aunt Margaret?" Just then the very same queen of clean charged into the room.

"Lizzy, for crying out loud ... have you looked at the clock? She'll be here in an hour." Then Aunt Margaret caught sight of me. "Peggy, did you change your sheets? And did you pull out all the dirty socks from under the bed? And what about that gunk stuck on your nightstand ... tell me you managed to scrape it off!"

"It's not gunk. I told you, it's my gum collection!" My aunt's eyes narrowed and Mom coughed nervously. "Yes, Aunt Margaret, I changed the sheets, put my smelly socks in the laundry, and left everything in my room spic-and-span, including the nightstand." She smiled skeptically and then tore off to the kitchen. It was tough living with my freakishly tidy Aunt Margaret and even worse when visitors came. At times like this even my mild-mannered Uncle Stewart made excuses to get out of the house and out of her way.

"Thank you, Peggy. I know it's not your thing, but making everything perfect for Great Aunt Beatrix's visit is important, especially to Aunt Margaret. Anything you can do to make it easier is appreciated."

It's hard to be mad at my mom. She's the kind of person who works really hard — even when she doesn't have to; always puts the needs of others first; and tiptoes around my nitpicky Aunt Margaret just to keep the peace. One thing's for certain — if Mom and I could afford a house of our own she would never sacrifice an entire Sunday to house cleaning.

"You go and do the bathroom while I get the good china down from the shelf," Mom suggested.

Now, cleaning the bathroom has got to be the worst chore in the world and under normal circumstances I'd complain about being asked to do it. But when Mom said the words *good china* a chill swept over me and I tore up the stairs as fast my legs could carry me. The china she was referring to was the blue and white porcelain dinner set Aunt Beatrix had passed down to my Aunt Margaret. It had been in the family for a zillion years and was only used on special occasions. It was displayed on top of a tall shelf in the dining room — a room we hardly ever went in. A room I happened to chase Duff into after school one day when we were playing a game of cat and mouse. When I accidentally chucked his catnip on top of the china cabinet he scooted up the curtain, then jumped over to retrieve it. That's when he suddenly met with the delicately patterned blue and white teapot, and some cups and saucers sitting on top. When it all came smashing to the floor I thought I would never breathe again. Fortunately for me there was no one else home and I had time to get out the glue. When the shattered pieces didn't stick right away I wrapped them with tape. I'd meant to go back and take it off but it wasn't long before I forgot all about the broken china ... that is until the very moment Mom mentioned getting it down from the shelf.

I ran into the bathroom and shut the door and braced myself for what was certain to be a scene involving a lot of screaming. That's when I remembered I'd forgotten to bring up the toilet scrubber and cleaning rags. There was no way I was going back down there and risk hastening a face-to-face confrontation. While I waited for the inevitable I looked under the sink for some cleaning supplies. There were only towels.

They would have to do. I used the brown towel on the toilet ... seemed the best choice. The pink one I used to wipe the sink and mirror, and then mopped the floor with it. All the while I waited for some kind of shriek that sounded like: PEGGY HENDERSON, GET YOUR BUTT DOWN HERE NOW! But it didn't come. Soon the bathroom was clean — well, at least it looked good to me. That's when I realized I'd have to do something with the dirty towels. I was sure Aunt Margaret wouldn't notice if I just neatly refolded them and put them back under the sink. That's just what I was doing when I heard Mom call my name — only her voice sounded rather sweet, not a hint of anger.

"Peggy, if you've finished cleaning the bathroom — properly — would you come down here and say hello to your Great Aunt Beatrix? She's arrived a little ... um ... early." I snickered when I thought about what was running through Aunt Margaret's mind. She was probably sweating over the dust still on the lampshades and the stacks of magazines in the hall.

"Okay, Mom — happy to!" I answered in an equally sweet voice — though I was sure Mom would recognize it as classic Peggy sarcasm.

When I got downstairs Mom whispered, "Did you do a good job?" I nodded. "Peggy?"

"Perfect — right down to folding the towels." I smiled as sincerely as possible. Just then I glanced over to the shelf in the dining room and noticed the broken china teapot was still perched at the top. I sighed with relief. They must have changed their minds about using it. *Bravo, Peggy — you dodged that bullet.* Suddenly feeling much happier than I thought I would, I bounced into the living room and found Great Aunt Beatrix sitting on the sofa.

"Hello, Aunt Beatrix," I blurted. At first she seemed startled and snorted at me in surprise. She was dressed in a green wool skirt that was tucked up under her well-endowed bosom and it gave the overall impression of her being some sort of human pear. At the end of her stubby arms were lots of silver bangles and her thin white hair was drawn up on the top of her head in a wispy bun.

"Oh, Peggy, you're so thin and tall." Was that supposed to be a compliment? "Now would that be the same hockey shirt you were wearing the last time we met?" I looked down at my slightly rumpled Canucks jersey with the ketchup stain.

"Yup, it's my favourite shirt." For some reason Mom's face turned the same shade of pink as the freshly cut peonies in the vase.

"And your hair … is that the way young people are styling their hair these days?"

I smoothed my hands over my messy hair. "What do you mean?"

"Well, it seems some girls have taken to colouring their hair purple, others have feathers … I just wondered if your mass of tangles was another new style."

"Naw, just didn't bother brushing it, that's all."

"Oh, I see. Well, I'm glad you didn't go to any trouble on my account." I noticed that Aunt Margaret was nervously picking at the pills on her sweater.

"Oh, I went to plenty of trouble on your account. Aunt Margaret had me up at seven o'clock scrubbing —"

"Aunt Beatrix," Aunt Margaret butted in. "I'm sure you must be ready for some refreshment after your long drive." I wondered why Aunt Margaret seemed to be on pins and needles around Great Aunt Beatrix. No matter to me really, I was just waiting for the right moment to make my escape.

TB and I were going for a bike ride down to Blackie's Spit. He's my best friend and has the dorkiest name on Earth — Thorbert. His dad named him that after some old Viking guy. When we met I could never say it with a straight face so I started calling him TB. Now everyone except his parents calls him that — I'm pretty sure it's a nickname that's saved him countless hours of teasing at school.

"The water is boiled. Should I make the tea?" called Uncle Stewart from the kitchen.

"Oh, I didn't get the teapot down yet," said Mom. "I'll do that right now." There was a sudden rush of blood to my face, and I felt dizzy.

"That would be delightful, Elizabeth. I so enjoy it when we have an opportunity to use the family heirloom china." Aunt Beatrix turned to me and scowled. "Peggy, dear, stop fidgeting with your fingernails. It isn't ladylike." I couldn't help myself. If she knew what was going to happen next she'd be fidgeting too. Then it came, a startling wail from the kitchen that sounded like the cat's tail had been banged in the cupboard door.

"Peggy, come in here — right now," Mom demanded from the kitchen.

"Oh dear, it sounds like we have a problem. Is there anything I can do?" Aunt Beatrix called. I gulped back my nervousness and wondered if I should make a run for it. I had taken two steps towards the front door when Aunt Margaret came into the room with a tear-streaked face.

"Peggy, don't you even think about it," Aunt Margaret said in a trembling voice. "You'll have to excuse us, Aunt Beatrix. We have a situation and need Peggy to clear it up." The blood that had suddenly rushed in now drained just as quickly from my face and I weakly followed my aunt to the kitchen.

"Perhaps I should make the tea while you take care of whatever it is," Great Aunt Beatrix offered. Aunt Margaret went even paler than me — if that was actually possible.

"No thank you, Aunt Beatrix. Your tea is on its way — won't be more than a couple of minutes." Aunt Margaret narrowed her eyes to two scary slits and pointed to the kitchen. When I walked in Mom was bent over the table peeling tape off of the teacups. When she glanced up I could see in her eyes that my life was in danger.

"Explain to me — and quickly — what happened to my china, Peggy? And don't even think of lying." I'd seen Aunt Margaret mad a lot of times, but never this bad.

"Well, one day after school Duff was all frisky, you see. He was tearing around the place like a crazy possessed maniacal —"

"Just get to the point," my aunt snapped.

"Like I was about to say ... he was tearing around when all of a sudden he latched onto the curtains and climbed up on the top of the shelf. That's when he knocked the china down." I decided for the time being it was best to leave off the part about me accidentally tossing his catnip up there. Since Duff was my aunt's cat I was pretty sure he'd be safe. It was my safety that I was worried about.

"Why didn't you say anything when it happened?" Aunt Margaret growled.

"Well, it was like five months ago." She gasped. "I thought maybe once the glue was set it would be okay. Then I forgot all about it." If there had been a club handy I sensed she would have used it. "It was an unfortunate accident, but let's get some perspective ... they're only dishes, and it's not like they ever get used." Another gasp, but this time it was from my mom.

"We don't use them because they're very valuable and old — well over a hundred years, in fact. We only use them for special occasions ... like this." Aunt Margaret's lips quivered. "They were given to me by Aunt Beatrix, who got them from her grandmother, and before that they came from some other distant relative. Do you realize how many generations these dishes go back?" I was in the process of doing the math, when Aunt Margaret fell onto the chair and started sobbing. "Aunt Beatrix expects us to serve tea in that teapot. Now what am I supposed to do?"

I started to offer some suggestions but Mom stopped me.

"Peggy, I don't want to hear it. You've completely missed the point here. This china means a lot to Aunt Margaret. She treasures it. I know an accident is an accident but it was irresponsible of you to not tell us about what happened. Not only is it a shame these dishes were broken, but you have put us in an awkward situation. I think you should go to your room and think about what you've done. And while you're there you'd better craft your apology speech and a have a plan for making amends." I hung my head and headed for the stairs.

"Stop," Aunt Margaret hissed. "You can't go there — it's Aunt Beatrix's room for now. Just ... just ... go outside. I don't want to see you right now."

Outside? I did my best to look like I detested the idea and shuffled to the back door. Then as soon as I could I scooted down the stairs and snatched my bike and helmet as fast as I could and rode off with the wind whistling past my ears.

That night I had a hard time sleeping, and it wasn't because of the lumpy sofa. First I'd been expelled from my room, and then I got reamed out over some crumby old broken teapot and cups, followed by Aunt Beatrix's snide observations about my sloppy posture and lack of fashion sense. If that wasn't bad enough, I got shrieked at again just before bed when Aunt Margaret found out the towels she gave Aunt Beatrix were the wet and dirty ones I'd used for cleaning the bathroom.

How was I going to survive two weeks of this? I needed to find a way to stay clear of Great Aunt Beatrix and Aunt Margaret. I was actually glad there was school the next day. Just then I remembered my class had a field trip in the morning to the Vancouver Maritime Museum. Maybe by the time I got home everyone would be calmed down.

"Welcome," beckoned a pretty young woman as we stepped inside the museum. Usually on museum field trips we got retired grandmothers who led the tours, but this one wasn't old at all, maybe mid-twenties. "I'm Amanda Marsh, your guide today here at the Vancouver Maritime Museum. If I can just get you to leave your bags here we'll get started in the main gallery by viewing the museum's pride and joy — the *St. Roch* — a schooner built a hundred years ago." We followed Amanda into a high ceilinged room filled from top to bottom with an old sailing ship. Its size took me by surprise and I felt dizzy looking up to the tip of the mast.

"How did they get this ship inside the building?" TB asked Amanda.

"They didn't put the ship in the building.

They built the building around it. A lot simpler, don't you think?" Amanda told us more about the *St. Roch*'s history, like how it used to be a Royal Canadian Mounted Police ship. Then we got to go aboard. As I looked over the deck and up to the top of the sails I thought about the sailing lessons I'd taken the summer before. We only got to sail tiny skiffs, but the instructor, Vic Torino, or the Tornado as we called him, had a really nice boat he took us sailing on. Even though he was a seriously weird guy, I did learn a lot of things, like how to maneuver the rudder and set the sail, how to read the gauges and maps, and mastered at least eight different kinds of knots.

As we toured the *St. Roch*, Amanda told us stories of adventure and danger of the old seafaring men of the past. We learned about Captain Cook and Captain Vancouver too. Vancouver surveyed and mapped the West Coast in the late 1700s. We learned that his navigational charts helped to open up the Pacific Ocean to a lot of other explorers and put the West Coast fur trade into high gear.

"Being an explorer was an adventurous lifestyle, but it was dangerous too and took men far from their homes and families for long periods of time," explained Amanda.

With everyone at home so mad at me, the idea of sailing away on a ship sounded like a good plan. Maybe not for months or years, but a couple of weeks would be nice. By the time I got back Great Aunt Beatrix would have gone home, the broken china forgotten, and things back to normal. Just then I had an idea. "Are we going to learn anything about sunken ships?" I asked.

Amanda smiled at my question. "You're jumping ahead of me, but as a matter of fact we are going to learn about a field of study that involves sunken ships. Can anyone tell me what archaeology is?"

Amanda's question caught me by surprise, but my hand shot up. When it comes to archaeology I'm practically an expert. That's because one of my best friends is an archaeologist. Her name is Dr. Edwina McKay, but I call her Eddy. I helped her with two professional investigations — the first involved digging up the remains of an ancient Coast Salish man in Crescent Beach where I live. And the second was rescuing a disturbed burial in the historic cemetery of Golden — it's one of those old railway towns in northern B.C. On top of that I'm a regular subscriber to *Dig* magazine and I'm a member of the Crescent Beach Archaeological Society.

"Archaeology uses things people made, or the places they lived and worked, or even their bodily remains to learn about humankind's past. These artifacts are often in the ground, so you have to dig them up — but not like you're digging for treasure. It has to be done carefully — there's a method to it."

"That's a great definition of archaeology," said Amanda. "So do archaeologists only recover artifacts in the ground?"

"Most often, although artifacts might also be found in places like caves or old temples or even out

in the open if the soil has eroded away." I was thinking of where I lived again. In Crescent Beach, lots of
people have found things that belonged to the early
Coast Salish right on the surface, like arrowheads,
hammerstones, and scrapers. It's not surprising since
they lived in the area for about five thousand years.

"So where do things like sunken ships fit in to
your definition?" Amanda asked. I admit I didn't
know much about how sunken ships and archaeology
went together. "Have you ever heard of underwater
archaeology? It's a branch of maritime archaeology."

TB snickered. "Looks like Indiana Jones Junior
still has a thing or two to learn," he whispered. If I
wasn't so keen on listening to Amanda I might have
planted a big red welt on the back of his neck as a
souvenir of our field trip.

"So just how do you dig under water?" I asked,
completely focused on this new idea. "Moving all
that sand and soil would make it pretty cloudy and
hard to see anything. And when you find artifacts
— how do they get to the surface without damage?
And what about properly recording the site?" I was
glad when Amanda laughed, because I could tell
that my teacher, Mrs. Sparrow, was about to hush
me for asking so many questions.

"It's nice to have a student who is so enthusias-
tic. And those are all good questions. For obvious
reasons excavating a maritime site is quite different
from those done on dry land. However, there are
several aspects that are the same. Like the site would
need to be surveyed and its position recorded, some

kind of a grid set out to mark the area of study, and in some cases sediment would need to be moved — perhaps by a special vacuum system that filters out the water but catches any objects sucked up. And because it's important to document and record as much information as possible, a good underwater camera and waterproof paper and pens come in handy." Then Amanda looked at me and winked. "Of course the first thing an underwater archaeologist would need to know is how to scuba dive."

By the time I got home that day I could tell the cat was out of the bag. Aunt Margaret was curt, Mom quiet, and Aunt Beatrix, who was drinking tea out of a mug, clicked her dentures resentfully the whole night until she went off to bed — my bed. But I didn't care because I'd had a great day. Even sleeping on the sofa couldn't spoil it. As I was dozing off I thought about what Amanda said about anyone serious about underwater archaeology would have to learn to dive. Tomorrow I'd pick Eddy's brain and then afterwards I'd figure out how to get Mom to let me take scuba diving lessons.

CHAPTER TWO

"If it's underwater archaeology that you're interested in you should meet my friend, Philip Hunter."
That's what Eddy said when I called the day after the
field trip to the Maritime Museum. Then just a few
days after that we were walking down the halls of the
archaeology department at Simon Fraser University
to meet him. As we passed open doors I got goose
bumps after catching glimpses of students and pro-
fessors working. In one room someone was hover-
ing over a tray of small broken pieces of pottery;
in another a lady was holding an aged bone in one
hand and comparing it to a similar one on a skeleton
hanging on a pole.

When we came to a closed door I read the
small name plate: Dr. Philip Hunter, Chairman,
Underwater Archaeology Department. My body
tingled as Eddy knocked.

"Hello, Edwina," the white-bearded man said
happily as he opened the door. "So good to see you.
And this must be the young lady you were telling
me about." I quickly glanced around Dr. Hunter's
office where there were wall-to-wall bookshelves
and a desk cluttered with stacks of papers, books,
and artifacts. On one wall hung a painting of an old

sailing ship and on the other an underwater photograph of a diver in clear green-blue water pointing to the decaying hull of a ship.

"Indeed it is, Philip. This is Peggy Henderson, my thirteen-year-old budding archaeologist and good friend. I thought you might be willing to fill us in on some of your recent work, Phil." My face prickled with warmth so I knew I was blushing.

"You know me, Edwina. I never pass up a chance to talk about my work. And since my wife, Katherine, rarely lets me anymore I'm always looking for a new audience." Eddy and her friend laughed. I didn't get it.

"Your wife's not interested in sunken ships or lost treasures? Is she nuts or something?" I blurted. The two adults snorted and chuckled some more.

"You have much to learn about relationships, young lady. One day you'll be married and know what I mean," he answered lightly. Right, like I would actually get tied down to someone not as interested in archaeology as I was.

Dr. Hunter soon began to tell us about his adventures exploring and excavating shipwrecks from all over the world. He helped to raise the *Resurgam II*, the first powered submarine, and a WWII merchant marine ship sunk by a U-boat in the Gulf of Mexico. But what was really interesting was hearing about the sixteenth-century British warship, the *Mary Rose*. He said it was the most famous shipwreck in the world. I wondered if he'd heard of the *Titanic*.

"Sunken ships are like time capsules to the past. But in the case of the *Mary Rose* — it was even more than that. It was a milestone in the field of maritime archaeology back in the 1980s. The most important things we know about underwater excavation and research we learned from excavating that ship. It was probably the most expensive project of its time, too."

"What caused the *Mary Rose* to sink?" I asked him.

"That's a good question. Some written records show the crew was especially unruly and hated one another so much that they refused to work cooperatively, perhaps even to the point of the ship's sinking. So crew error may certainly have been part of the cause. Other theories include, she was overloaded after being fitted with extra cannons; an especially strong wind caught her in a turn; or a French cannon smashed her hull. The sinking of the *Mary Rose* is one of those events that we'll likely never know for sure what the real cause was."

He pointed to a large book on his shelf called *The Mary Rose*. "We did make some spectacular finds though. The cannons and shot gave us a good glimpse into eighteenth-century naval warfare, the eating utensils and food remains helped us to know a little of how they lived. And the navigational and medical instruments revealed something of the technology of the day."

"That's interesting indeed. I imagine determining the cause of a shipwreck that occurred in past centuries must be very difficult," Eddy added.

"That's true, Edwina, though we do get lucky once in a while." At that moment Dr. Hunter's eyes began to twinkle.

"By the grin on your face I have the feeling you're about to share one of those lucky cases."

"I will if you think you can keep it to yourself." Dr. Hunter looked long at me. "If this gets out to the media prematurely it could ruin everything. We don't want a flock of treasure hunters getting in there and wrecking what could possibly be the most important shipwreck find in recent history. So if you're good at keeping secrets, I have something extraordinary to tell you about."

"I'm good at keeping my mouth shut," I blurted excitedly. "I would keep your secret even if I was being tortured."

Eddy snorted and nodded. "It's true ... even torture won't make her talk when she puts her mind to it."

"All right then, if you're sure you won't tell. Last week a fisherman was out past Tlatskwala, also known as Trust Island. It's off the north coast of Vancouver Island near Port Hardy. His net got caught up on something and he called for a diver to come out and try to free it. The diver went down about fifty feet and discovered what the net was snagged on." I didn't realize it until that moment, but I'd stopped breathing and took a big gulp of air. "It was over-grown with barnacles and seaweed, but there was no mistaking it for a late eighteenth-century anchor. Once the diver freed the net he took it on his own initiative to look around. Though the water was murky, it didn't take him too long to notice a few scattered objects, such as the cathead — the part of the ship where the anchor would have been secured, a pulley, and a broken mast." My heartbeat raced as I slipped to the edge of my chair.

"So did he find the rest of the ship?" I asked, impatient to hear the next part of the story.

"Well, no. By then his oxygen tank was running low, so with that and a storm warning he decided to get back to the surface. Fortunately for us he called the department instead of the news stations," Dr. Hunter said. Then he pointed to the painting of the old fashioned ship with three sails. "From historical records we know there was a ship like this one that sank in that area in 1812 and belonged to John Jacob Astor's American Fur Company. It was called the *Intrepid* and it too was a three-mast bark. While we won't know for sure until we go there and have a look for ourselves, there's a very good possibility that it's the *Intrepid*. And if it is, that will be a very big deal."

When Dr. Hunter finished the room was silent. I couldn't think of a single intelligent thing to say besides, "Wow." Then Eddy broke the silence.

"So what's next, Phil?"

"I'm putting together a team of underwater archaeologists who can join me on a preliminary investigation. We have to get in there as quick as possible and establish a presence before some rogue shipwreck treasure hunters. If they get a hold of this there's no telling what damage they might do. Presuming this is the *Intrepid* we'll want to time our announcement to the media just right. After that …" He chuckled. "I'm sure funding will come flooding in to pay for a full-on excavation. Amateur shipwreck divers love to support these kinds of investigations and in my line of business this is as good as winning the Lotto 649 Jackpot. Depending on her condition we may want to try and raise her from the ocean floor and bring her back for preservation." He sat back, looking very pleased. "So now you know what we're dealing with and why we need to keep this quiet."

Dr. Hunter handed Eddy a large folder. "That's a photocopy of the original journal kept by the captain of the ship — Captain James Whittaker." She flipped through it and handed it to me. I held it in my hand like it was some kind of sacred holy book. I leafed through it, but it was hard to read the old-fashioned cursive writing with its fancy scratches and swirls.

"So how did the journal survive if the ship sank?" I asked.

"The ship sank slowly and that gave the captain time to make a final entry while his crew boarded the lifeboats. From it, we know there was barely enough room for the entire crew. This must be why the captain made the decision to stay with the ship. He gave his journal to his first mate to deliver to Astor in the event that they made it back to New York City alive — which obviously they did. And that's why today we know so much about the *Intrepid*."

"You said the captain stayed with the ship. Why did he do that?"

"Captain Whittaker was one of those rare breed of men for whom commitment, honour, and responsibility ran deep. It has long been the standard amongst seamen that the captain's responsibility was to save the lives of the crew, the ship, and the cargo if possible." I thought about the cruise ship *Costa Concordia* that struck huge rocks in the Mediterranean a few years back, which tore open the hull. In that case as soon as the ship started listing, Captain Schettino was one of the first to abandon ship. Sadly, many passengers were not able to get off and died. Clearly Schettino missed the memo about a captain being the last to leave a sinking ship.

"So if the captain couldn't fit in the lifeboat why didn't he at least try to swim to shore?"

"Like many sailors of that day, the captain couldn't swim," Dr. Hunter said. Now that was dumb. Fortunately my Mom insisted I learn to swim when I was a little kid.

"So when do you think you'll go up to check her out?" asked Eddy. That was what I wanted to know too.

"Soon … very soon. We have already started getting the crew and equipment together. So the next thing is to do an assessment — for that we need to find the anchor, the ship, and its contents. We could be on our way in a few weeks. Care to join us, Dr. McKay?" Eddy smiled, but shook her head no.

"I'd love to, but I'm afraid I've got too much

work to do, and then there's my grandson's sixth birthday party. I know someone else who'd be happy to go, though." Eddy looked at me and my mind started jumping around like popcorn in a hot pot.

"Do you scuba dive, Peggy?" asked Dr. Hunter.

I was so eager that I jumped off the chair. "Well sir, I've already signed up for lessons and start tomorrow." I hoped Eddy couldn't see my neck and ears. Mom said they always turned red when I was making stuff up. But what harm was there in saying something when it was going to be true soon enough ... that is right after I figured out how to get Mom to agree to letting me take lessons. "I'm sure I'll have my Level 1 certification by the time we're ready to go, sir — that is if I'm allowed to join you."

"And your parents, what would they say about you going off to search for a sunken ship?"

"Well, I don't have a dad. He died a long time ago." Before Dr. Hunter had time to say he felt sorry for me, I added: "That's okay, I'm used to it. And my mom, well she loves stuff like this, right Eddy?" Now if I had to share what Aunt Margaret would think, I'd be sunk like the *Intrepid*. Dr. Hunter was quiet and rubbed his chin — I think he was trying to decide if taking a kid was such a good idea. I needed to sweeten the deal. "If it will help — I'll swab the deck, furl the sails, and even act as shark bait if I have to." The corner of his eyes wrinkled and he laughed softly.

"Shark bait, eh? That could be handy." I hoped he knew I was kidding. "Well, let's see, shall we? One thing is for sure, you'll need that diving certificate.

And you better get some practice diving in open water. It's no good to us if all you know how to do is scuba dive in a pool."

"Aye aye, Captain." If I could I would have done a back flip and squealed like a piglet. Instead I saluted him.

"Dr. McKay, you'd better be right about this young lady ... I haven't made anyone walk the plank for some time, but I'm not above it should there be a need."

The drive home was agonizing. All I wanted to do was jump and dance and yelp, but instead I was strapped into the car seat. I mean how lucky could I be? Me, Peggy Henderson, sailing off on an adventure to find a two-hundred-year-old sunken ship. *Wait until TB hears about this! Indiana Jones Junior is moving up the ladder ... or should I say down the ladder?* The first thing I had to do was get Mom to let me take scuba diving lessons.

I had hoped everyone would be in a good mood when I got home. Instead Aunt Margaret was fuming — again, Uncle Steward was hiding out in the TV room, and Aunt Beatrix was madly polishing the silverware. I soon found out Mom had to stay late at work and I would have to survive Friday evening the best I could without her.

"Homework, on a Friday evening? My, that's ambitious of you. Are you sure you don't have time to watch *Reach for the Top* with me? It's very educational," urged Aunt Beatrix.

"Sounds good," I lied. "But I've got some stuff I've got to do." Doing homework was my excuse for finding a quiet place where I could start cooking up my plan for getting Mom to first agree to let me have diving lessons and then to go with Dr. Hunter to search for the *Intrepid*.

It was after ten o'clock when I finally got to crawl into my sleeping bag on the living room sofa with the books Dr. Hunter had loaned me. *The Great West Coast Fur Trade* was a book about Captain James Cook, the first explorer to set foot on what is now British Columbia in 1778. He traded trinkets, beads, knives, blankets, and other stuff for otter furs with the coastal First Nations. Then he sailed to China where he was able to sell the furs for other stuff. That was the beginning of the Pacific fur trade, which went until the 1830s.

The other book I dug into was *Nautical and Underwater Archaeology for the Beginner*. I learned that nautical archaeology was concerned with all the things to do with trade routes, navigational techniques, harbours, boats, fishing equipment, and stuff like that, while underwater archaeology was mostly sunken sites, like shipwrecks.

I was starting to get sleepy and my eyes wanted to close, but I just couldn't go to sleep without at least reading the first few pages of Captain Whittaker's journal. His chicken-scratch handwriting was hard to decipher, but I soon got used to the style.

* * *

October 3rd, 1811

After loading the Intrepid *with the last of her stores, we put out to sea today with a fair wind. Our cargo consists of such things as fine English cloths and Dutch blankets, looking glasses, tinware and copper pots, and razors and knives for trading with the natives. Also aboard are great quantities of ammunition, cutlasses, pistols, and muskets for the Russians. We have about twenty hogsheads of rum, including stores for the ship and some sugar and molasses as well.*

Our journey will take us first to St. Catherine's Island, off the coast of Brazil, where we shall stop for a few days to wood, water, and take on fresh provisions. Once we have our supplies replenished it is my hope that we set sail immediately. If all goes well, the Intrepid *should round Cape Horn before Christmas. The voyage will be warm and easy sailing through the Sandwich Islands, though rougher seas await us when we make our way north. Nevertheless, this gives me no discomfort as the* Intrepid *is a fine bark with three sails, six guns, and as spacious and solid a ship as any I ever captained in my career. As we travel north we will trade for otter furs. Once the ship is filled we set sail across the Pacific for the land of tea and china.*

It was a tremendous honour to have Mister Astor himself attend our departure in New York harbour and with his usual flair he waved us off. I am most pleased to have Mister John Carver aboard again as my first mate. He's sure to be a fine captain himself one day. We have three French Canadians, hired by

Mister Astor himself for their expertise in the fur trade. We also have a full complement of Brits and my own countrymen, whom I selected for their steely nerve and hearty dispositions.

There is one other soul aboard. He is one of Mister Astor's business partners — Mister Robert Lockhart is a Scotsman from Lower Canada. He will oversee the trading, while I am to be left without interference to captain the Intrepid. *I have observed that the man has peculiar habits when relating to the crew and I must report that thus far his encounters are less than favourable. Yesterday when introducing himself he attempted to set his authority by threatening the men. He stated that any man found not to be fully loyal to the American Fur Company would be left on the first island, inhabited or not. In my long career I have found that the loyalty of a good seaman must be won by firm and fair leadership and not threats intended to frighten him into submission. Mister Lockhart must learn these are not schoolboys, but fierce sailors who have weathered the worst the sea has to offer. I shall endeavor to impart this wisdom in the coming weeks.*

At 7 o'clock this evening, Mister Carver brought his report to my cabin and mentioned there was a peculiar ring around the moon — he said it was perhaps a sign of coming bad weather. I know many seamen who are slaves to superstition and think this may be a bad omen, but I have no such fears. While on my walkabout later the clouds had already rolled in and nary the moon nor the stars could be seen. We are prepared for rain in the morning and perhaps there will be a storm by noon. This is not what we desired for our second day at sea, but since the Intrepid *is such a solid bark I am certain it can weather anything.*

Captain James Whittaker

CHAPTER THREE

"So I've been thinking, Aunt Margaret," I said at breakfast the next morning. "I'm sorry about the china and I want to make it up to you." Mom beamed at me while Aunt Margaret's eyes narrowed — pretty much what I expected.

"This plan of yours — it's going to make up for a broken heirloom that's almost a hundred and fifty years old?" Aunt Margaret asked dryly.

That old, eh? I could understand why she was peeved.

"Margie, let's just hear what she has in mind," Mom said. I started out carefully.

"I'll bet keeping Aunt Beatrix entertained all day has been a pain — am I right?" Mom shot me a look about the same time as Aunt Margaret frowned. "Don't get me wrong ... she's probably been a pain in a nice way." My speech wasn't coming out like I had rehearsed in my mind. "Anyway, I was thinking you might like some time off, so how about I do stuff with her sometimes?"

"You'll do stuff with her? Like what?" Aunt Margaret asked doubtfully.

"You know, I could show her around Crescent Beach. I could tell her about the ancient Coast Salish who once lived here. We could visit Mr. Grimbal's store. Maybe I could show her how to tie sailor's knots and how to play Crazy Eights. It'll be fun."

Mom and Aunt Margaret looked at each other and I could tell they were talking with their eyes the way sisters do when they know exactly what the other one is thinking. Then they both started to do that snort giggle thing that runs in the family. Why did I have the feeling that maybe I should have thought this through more? I knew Aunt Beatrix was bossy and opinionated, but just how bad could it be spending time with her?

"Good morning, everyone. What's all this joviality about?" Great Aunt Beatrix came through the kitchen doorway. She was wearing a huge nightgown that flowed around her like a floral tent and her thin white hair was wound up tight in pink curlers. I didn't think people used those things anymore.

"Peggy, don't you have school today?" she said when she finally took note of me.

"Nope, it's Saturday. Remember, Aunt Beatrix?" She sighed heavily at me. What was that about? She was the one who couldn't seem to keep the days of the week straight.

"Peggy, please don't say 'nope.' You need to speak proper English during your formative years; otherwise you will develop poor grammar habits." I bit my lip to hold in the groan. "And dear, don't you think you'd better put something else on?" She turned to Mom, whose cheeks had turned pink. "Really Elizabeth, you can't approve of this. She's worn that shirt two days in a row. And shouldn't she do something with her hair?" I felt my mussed-up hair, then looked down at my Canucks jersey. It had only a couple of dirty smudges, but otherwise was perfectly fine.

"Actually it's the fourth day that I've worn this shirt, Aunt Beatrix. And unless something drastic happens to it today, I'll probably wear it tomorrow too." I watched her baggy eyelids widen. Aunt Margaret nervously brushed at the crumbs on the table and Mom quietly slipped out of her chair and took the dishes to the sink.

"Oh, I see. Well, in my day, children were expected to be clean and dressed appropriately. But …" She sighed. "… those days are gone. You youngsters go around with rings in your noses and eyebrows, and your arms marked up with tattoos, and wear the most atrocious things." She looked at my jersey with her nose all wrinkled … like it smelled or something. That was the moment when I figured out what Mom and Aunt Margaret were laughing about earlier.

"Right, well, that's very interesting. But I'm off to the library." I saw my mom's eyes widen. I bet she knew I was already working on how to get out of spending time with the old biddy. I needed to come up with a different plan to get those diving lessons. Just then Aunt Margaret opened her big mouth.

"By the way, Aunt Beatrix, you'll be pleased to know that Peggy is planning to spend some time with you this afternoon and on school days when she gets home. In fact, it was her idea. So now the two of you can get to know each other better. Won't that be nice?" The look in my Aunt Margaret's eyes told me I'd walked right into the quicksand and she had no plans to rescue me. I jumped out of my chair and headed quickly for the back door.

"Gotta go," I said, and whipped out the door. On the way out I heard the last of their conversation.

"Well, that's wonderful. I'm very sure with daily guidance I can set Peggy on the right course — just as I did when you both were girls."

Great! While I thought I'd come up with the perfect plan for softening Mom up so I could get diving lessons, in actual fact I had become an improvement project for my great aunt.

I stayed out as long as I could. First, I stopped at the library to look for books on underwater archaeology. When the librarian couldn't find anything she offered me a book on some old guy named Jacques Cousteau. She said he was famous because he explored the oceans and was like the father of scuba diving. I figured it was worth a look. My next stop was TB's house to use his computer to locate the Reef Dive Shop and find out about lessons — it was the nearest dive shop to home, and the best part was they had beginner lessons starting almost every week.

When I finally got home Aunt Beatrix was sitting at the kitchen table wearing her coat with the fur collar and some crazy-ugly brown shoes. On her head was a dorky feather hat. She must have been hot, which would explain the serious scowl on her pinched face.

"I was beginning to wonder if you were ever going to come," Aunt Beatrix said curtly. "I was led to believe we would be going out this afternoon. If I'd known you were going to return so late I would have gone with your mother and Margaret. You know it's very rude to keep people waiting." She made an exaggerated effort to look at her watch. "I'm not even sure now if I have the energy for an outing anymore ..." Brilliant, that suited me just fine. "... But I suppose I can muster the strength for a short excursion. Perhaps to that gift shop that sells antiques and aboriginal art. What's it called?"

"Real Treasures and Gifts," I sighed.

"Yes, that's the place. Well, let's get going then." She shooed me out the door like a little kid with muddy feet.

All the way to Beecher Street Aunt Beatrix nattered on at me like a cranky parrot. Mostly it was about the broken china. She reminded me it had been in the family for six generations and that one day it might be mine. "If there's anything left of it, that is," she said. After a while she moved on to my dirty fingernails and torn sneakers. She'd just started giving me tips about the best way to make a good impression on my teachers when we finally arrived at Real Treasures and Gifts. I was trying to estimate how much trouble I'd get in if I just dumped her off on Mr. Grimbal and ran for it. He was just as crusty as Aunt Beatrix so they'd make a great pair.

"Hello ladies, come right in," Mr. Grimbal said in his slick, used-car salesman voice. "And who is this charming lady with the elegant hat, Peggy?" Oh please, did he think that kind of goopy flattery actually worked? Then Aunt Beatrix giggled daintily. Hmmm, obviously he knew something I didn't.

"Good afternoon, sir. What an interesting shop you have. Now you must tell me about these objects — are they all made by First Nations?" I could tell Mr. Grimbal was already sizing up Aunt Beatrix's wallet and wondering if he should start with the expensive stuff.

"What a fascinating man Mr. Grimbal is," Aunt Beatrix gushed as we walked back home. "Such a pity he doesn't have a wife to help him. He's just the kind of man I can relate to — educated, polite, and a successful businessman too. I do hope we'll come visit him again, Peggy." Gross! It sounded like Aunt Beatrix had something in mind besides shopping for souvenirs at Mr. Grimbal's store.

All through dinner Aunt Beatrix chatted on happily about Mr. Grimbal, his store, and the ancient Coast Salish — she didn't even mention that I was late picking her up. I was actually impressed with how much she'd learned and remembered. And I could tell Mom and Aunt Margaret were pleased with her chipper mood. That meant serious brownie points for me.

"Aunt Beatrix seemed thrilled with her outing today, Peggy," said Mom at bedtime. Maybe this was all going to work in my favour after all. When she was finished gushing her appreciation I'd bring up the topic of scuba diving lessons. "It might well be the highlight of her trip. And it was a big help to Aunt Margaret too, as she had some important errands to get done."

"It was my pleasure," I lied. Then with a soft tone and as little eye contact as possible I added, "Mom, ah, there's something I want to talk to you about." Mom didn't have a lot of extra cash and we were always on a tight budget — one that I'm sure didn't include diving lessons. "TB was thinking since he lives right on one of the world's most beautiful coasts it would be a cool thing if he learned to scuba dive. His mom really likes the idea and thought if I took lessons with him it would give him more confidence — you know, because he's not as good a swimmer as I am. I told her that you probably couldn't afford it, but that I'd ask you anyways."

I twisted the details of my story as though I was tying a back hitch knot. I knew Mom was proud and didn't like others to think she couldn't afford to give me all the same advantages in life that kids with two parents got. So in a way I was doing her a favour.

"I wish you wouldn't tell people that I can't afford things. It gives a wrong impression." Then she gazed up to the ceiling like she was calculating something in her mind. After a few minutes of silence she looked at me. "How important is this to you, Peggy? It has to be something you want to do for yourself and not just because TB is taking scuba lessons." I jumped up and down on the sofa excit-edly and held out my arms wide.

"I really want to learn to scuba dive, Mom." Then I settled myself back down on the sofa and put on my pious face again. "But not if we can't afford it." *Nailed it.*

"Well, I have been saving some money for a new computer, but I guess I can get along with the old one for a while longer. I don't mind as long as you're sure this is something you'd really benefit from." I leapt off the sofa.

"It will be the best thing in the world," I blurted. "Thanks, Mom."

"Just don't forget that you promised you'd do things with your great aunt."

"You bet — even if it kills me."

The next morning I told TB all about my plan and the little lie I'd told. "So what about it, why don't you see if you can take diving lessons too?" He stared at me for a few moments with a blank look and then his face suddenly lit up.

"That's a brilliant idea. I always imagined myself a Jacques Cousteau kind of guy."

"You know about him?"

"What, Cousteau? Well, duh. He's only like the father of scuba diving and underwater exploration."

"Yup, good old Jack."

"Jacques, you mean."

"Right. So anyway, are you sure your mom will let you?"

"Peggy, one of the few benefits of having divorced parents is when one says no, you can almost always count on the other saying yes."

"Great. I'm going to sign up after school at the Reef Dive Shop."

"I thought you were doing something with your Great Aunt Beatrix today." Shoot, I'd forgotten about that.

"Hey, TB. Help me out here. Phone my house and tell my aunt that you need me to come over so we can get started on that important school project that's due next Friday."

"What important school project?" he said with panic in his eyes.

"There is no project dough-head. I just want you to say that so when I walk in the house and Aunt Beatrix gives me your message she won't think anything when I tell her I can't spend time with her today."

"Sorry, Peggy. I don't like lying — especially to adults. From my experience I always get caught or end up making matters worse. You'll have to get out of this one on your own." If he hadn't been my best friend I'd have given him a raspberry somewhere embarrassing.

When I got home, there she was — Queen Bee-atrix — in her hat and waiting to go out. "Peggy, you're slouching, stand up straight, dear." I did everything to keep myself from groaning out loud. "So, where shall we wander today, dear? Mr. Grimbal suggested we take a stroll through Heron Park and have a look at the stone carvings — petroglyphs, I think he called them. It sounds delightfully primitive." I sighed dramatically. "What? Doesn't that sound like a good plan to you?"

"Oh, it's not that, Aunt Beatrix. I definitely want to go see the petroglyphs with you. I'm just trying to figure out how I can do that and get my assignment done for school."

"Assignment for school?"

"Yah, my friend TB and I have to make a diorama by tomorrow of Captain Vancouver's voyage along the Pacific Coast." There it was again, the perfect lie rolling effortlessly off my tongue. "Oh well, never mind, I'll just call TB and tell him I can't do it …"

"You'll do no such thing. Getting homework assignments completed is absolutely paramount, Peggy. If there is anything I can teach you, it's to take your work seriously and live up to your commitments. Now you get to it right now, do you hear young lady?" I nodded as though I was completely disappointed and about to object.

It didn't take me long to scoot out the door, hop on my bike, and make my way towards the dive shop. I had mom sign the permission sheet that morning and write out a cheque to pay for the lessons. I pedalled as fast I could up the steep hill towards Ocean Park. I was hot when I got there but the moment I walked inside the dive shop I got goose bumps. Dangling from hooks were wet suits, masks, snorkels, and other gear. There was a guy there trying on flippers too.

"Man, these are perfect. I'm going to whiz around like a dolphin in these," he said to the clerk. Just then she caught sight of me.

"Here to sign up for lessons?"

I nodded and held out the form and cheque.

"Great, I'll just add your name to our list. We have a new set of lessons starting next week. But if you're eager you can start tomorrow — we still have a few spots open in our four o'clock class." My heart leapt.

"The sooner the better," I sang out. "Put my name on the list for sure." Not only was I going to start scuba diving lessons in less than twenty-four hours, I had the perfect excuse for no longer being able to spend time entertaining Aunt Beatrix after school.

When I rode into the yard I could tell it was nearly dinnertime from all the clanging going on in the kitchen. Uncle Stewart was watering the plants.

"Hi Uncle Stu, what's up?"

"Oh, your Aunt Margaret for one thing," he whispered. "She's wound up tight as a top. Sure would've helped if you'd taken Aunt Beatrix out."

"But I had to —" I started to explain, but he gave me the hush signal.

"Save it, Pegs. I'm just saying it would have been helpful." I had a brief moment of feeling guilty.

"I could teach you how to tie some sailor's knots, Aunt Beatrix," I said after supper. My gesture was really a peace offering to Aunt Margaret. I held out the silky strands I used for practicing my sailor's knot tying, but the old bat shook her head.

"No, thank you."

"Okay, how about we play Crazy Eights?" That time she sighed and gave me one of those faint smiles that really meant don't bother me, kid. *All right*, I thought, *how about if I let you nag me about my hair some more and point out all my other weaknesses?* "Any chance you'd like to teach me something?" I offered in a final attempt. I thought my efforts had been admirable, and everyone had seen me try. Fortunately she'd turned down all my ideas and I was about to split for the living room to watch TV. That's when Aunt Beatrix caught me by the arm.

"Teach you something? Now there's an idea!" I could tell she'd just remembered I was her improvement project. "There is something I can teach you — something every young lady should know how to do." She turned to Aunt Margaret. "Now Margaret dear, I don't want you to fret — though I know you have good reason to — but I'd like to teach this child the value of your precious china set. She will start by learning how to set the table properly." I watched Aunt Margaret's eyes pop out.

"Oh, Aunt Beatrix, do you think —"

"No, no. It will be fine dear. I will see to it."

Oh no, what did I get myself into?

For the next hour Great Aunt Beatrix taught me the finer details of how to set the table — informally for those frequent occasions when it's just close friends and family; then formally for the times when I might want to impress my husband's boss — yah right; and then for those special once-in-a-lifetime events when someone important — like, let's say Her Royal Highness, Queen of England — should decide to drop in and dine with me. Aunt Beatrix was on a roll and I zoned in and out until Mom rescued me.

"Bedtime, Peggy. You've got school in the morning." I leapt off the sofa and was about to make a run for it.

"Quite right, young lady. Just let me conclude this lesson by saying that setting an elegant table is more than it appears. It's symbolic that even in your day-to-day existence it's possible to be careful, orderly, gracious, and temperate. And as you take more care in the smallest details of your life you'll find when the going gets tough, you'll be able to stay the course, face up to your problems with courage, and remain honest and true. If nothing else, remember it's your moment-by-moment conduct that will determine the success of your life. So always put your best foot forward, Peggy. Give your all to everything you do and never run away from your problems." Before she could add another word I scrambled up the stairs to get into my pj's and brush my teeth.

By the time I got back to the living room Mom had my bed made up on the sofa.

"That was sweet of you, Peggy. Aunt Beatrix always feels so good when she thinks she's been useful." I put my hands to my neck and pretended to choke myself. Mom laughed. "Huh, you think that was tough. That's nothing. Aunt Margaret and I have a whole lifetime of lessons like that. But even so, we love Aunt Beatrix. She has a good heart and believe it or not, lots of the things she taught have come in handy — even how to set the table nicely." Mom kissed me goodnight and headed up the stairs. "Oh, by the way, Aunt Beatrix hopes you'll take her to see the petroglyphs tomorrow. I told her I was sure you'd be ecstatic!" I heard her giggle after she'd turned off the light. I groaned and flung the pillow at her. Aunt Beatrix may want to see Heron Park tomorrow, but I was starting scuba diving lessons. I also needed to come up with the second part of my plan — how to make sure Mom let me go on the search for the *Intrepid*.

Happy to finally have time to myself I snuggled down in the sleeping bag and opened Captain Whittaker's journal.

October 18th, 1811

By all estimates we shall reach St. Catherine's in a fortnight. It will do us all good to get off the ship and stretch our legs. The island is a serviceable destination to take on fresh supplies, for it abounds with plantains, oranges and bananas, and abundant good spring water. I have ordered Mister Carver to stock us with enough to reach the Sandwich Islands. The last time I made this same voyage it took us nearly a month to sail round the Horn for the winds were fierce and tempestuous and drove us back nearly two hundred miles. If luck be on our side we will get past her before winter sets in.

We have on board a fine band of musicians and they play most nights. This is a great source of comfort for us all. Besides singing and dancing the men occupy themselves in the evenings with card playing, chess, and a few of the lads who are able enjoy reading. There are some who would like it very much should I allow more consumption of rum and gambling. However, since the voyage when we lost our master gunner, who threw himself overboard when he had gambled away a year's pay and his father's pocket watch, I have kept the spirits and gambling to a minimum.

I am pleased to see an alliance has sprung up between one of my young clerks, Mister Albert Smedley and Mister Lockhart. The boy was educated in Brighton and as such is good company for the gentleman. The two frequently engage in lively discussions at mealtime. Most recently I enjoyed their debate regarding Niccolo Machiavelli's The Art of War — *Smedley much more the pacifist than the other gentleman. Nevertheless, perhaps this new friendship is evidence that Lockhart is finally settling into the rhythm of sea life. Should this be the case it would put my mind at rest.*

I have made a point to remind Cook to set out the salt dish at mealtimes. I prefer it as a savory over the salt water he uses, which seems to make the meat tough.

Captain James Whittaker

October 27th, 1811

I recently learned that my boatswain, Mister Douglas, had forfeited an entire month's pay over a gambling debt. It is in fact the second such incident in recent days and in each case it seems there was a liberal outpouring of cheap gin that preceded the gaming. It is a well known fact that Mister Douglas cannot hold his liquor nor afford to lose a month's pay, what with a family of seven at home. When I learned of the loss I was indeed very angry and immediately sought out my first mate, Mister Carver. He conducted a brief investigation and learned that it was Mister Lockhart who not only provided the men with excessive gin, but is the man to whom Mister Douglas was indebted.

Mister Lockhart's actions constitute treachery and are a threat to the success of this voyage. Out of respect for Mister Astor, I chose to approach the matter as a gentleman. When Lockhart appeared before me I strongly suggested he release Mister Douglas from his debt. At this the man scoffed at me heartily, saying such action would undermine the men's respect for him and he would never be able to command them. At this I reminded him that it was my job to command the crew and his to oversee the trading. He was mildly contrite and agreed never to give them liquor without my specific permission. He did not yet commit to releasing Mister Douglas from the debt.

A note to self: Instruct Mister Carver to convey to the crew the need to wash their bodies more regularly. Besides the innocuous odour, I wish to see them remain healthy and fit for the duration of the voyage.

Captain James Whittaker

Monday morning I woke feeling queasy — almost like I was seasick. When I rolled out of bed I forgot I was on the sofa and landed on the floor with a loud thunk. Mom poked her head into the living room.

"You okay, kiddo?"

"Groannnnn! Other than the fact that my back hurts from this coil in the sofa poking me all night, and cramps in my legs from not being able to stretch them out, and an upset stomach — I guess you could say I'm hunky-dory."

"Good. I left cereal on the table for you. I'm just going to dive into the shower and when I'm finished you can have the bathroom. Okay?" I nodded sleepily and was about to get back under the covers. Wait — did she say "dive"? I sat up abruptly, forgetting all my aches and pains.

"Yahoo! I start diving lessons today." Mom's head shot around the corner.

"What? Did you say you're starting diving lessons today?" Oh right, I'd decided to put off telling her yesterday about the start date to avoid setting Aunt Margaret off again … who for some reason was determined now that I take Aunt Beatrix off her hands every day. "Sorry Mom, the plan changed a bit. TB has something he has to do later in the month so we had to start this week. My lessons are at four o'clock." Mom plunked down on the sofa looking dazed.

"I'm sorry I won't be able to entertain Aunt Beatrix after school today. It's just too bad she has to leave next weekend. I was starting to enjoy getting to know her."

"Really? Well, I'm glad you feel that way. I did notice how well the two of you get on." Was she blind? It was just out of necessity that I let the old bird boss me around and teach me useless stuff like table setting. But soon she'd be gone and I'd be off the hook. I began folding up the sleeping bag.

"Actually, Peggy, yours aren't the only plans that have changed. You know how Aunt Margaret and Uncle Stewart have been thinking of taking that Caribbean cruise for a long time, but the timing just never seemed right? Well, they are finally doing it … and they leave this Saturday for three weeks."

"This Saturday? That's great," I chirped. Now I knew why she was so busy and stressed lately. Then I realized three weeks without Aunt Margaret on my heels would be like having my own holiday.

"Yes, it is great. They so deserve something like this after all they've done for us. And the reason we all feel so free about them going is knowing you won't be home alone waiting for me to get back from work."

"Right, because I'll be taking scuba diving lessons."

"Actually, no, it's because Aunt Beatrix has agreed to stay on." I jumped off the seat and hit my knee on the coffee table.

"Ouch!" I yelped. "Mom, what were you thinking? I don't need a babysitter." How could they think I needed looking after — and of all people they chose the Grim Reaper of children? "I repeat, Mom, what were you thinking?"

"You just said how it was too bad she wasn't staying longer. And besides, it's not all about you. She'll be able to get the meals started, keep Duff company, and be here if you should — as completely unlikely as it could be — get into trouble and need help. And on the bright side, you'll have scuba lessons to focus on and you'll get your room back after Aunt Beatrix moves into Margaret's room."

The bright side, right! How was I ever going to survive another month with the only person in the world more uptight than Aunt Margaret? This is exactly the kind of thing that could give a kid nightmares or a nervous tick. Just then I remembered the trip to find the *Intrepid*. School would be finished and maybe if I just played along with all this I'd have a better chance of getting Mom's permission to go with Dr. Hunter and his research team. I took a deep breath, counted to ten, and then quickly shifted gears.

"Okay, Mom. That's cool." I could tell my sudden change of attitude surprised her.

"It's cool? Well, good. Quite honestly I thought you'd put up more of a fuss, but I guess this means you're growing up, and getting more mature."

"Sure, that's it, Mom. I'm just getting more mature."

CHAPTER FOUR

TB got the okay to start scuba lessons with me. So the plan was for me to stop off at home after school to say hello to Aunt Beatrix for five minutes — Mom's idea, not mine — and then ride to the pool with him. But when Mrs. Sparrow kept me in to discuss my poor score on the English test I had to let him go ahead on his own and skip going home. By the time I got there the other students were already in their gear and sitting on the edge of the pool. As I walked over to the group I heard a voice from somewhere in my past. I couldn't quite place it until I saw him.

"No, it can't be," I cursed. By the look on TB's face he knew what I meant. Just then the diving instructor looked up at me. Yup, it was none other than the face of Vic Torino, a.k.a. the Tornado, my sailing instructor from last summer. He hadn't changed a bit — still tall, skinny, and tanned so dark and shiny he looked like an oily hot dog fresh off the BBQ.

"Late for the first class, eh? Not a good sign, man. You know what they say about punctuality — it's the early worm that catches the bird." A few of the students tittered. I looked at TB, who was doing his best to muffle his laughter.

"Don't you mean it's the early bird who catches the worm?" I answered, trying not to laugh myself.

"Well, whatever, it's a virtue to be on time, right?"

"True, but you know what they also say — better late than never." I could see he was trying to add that one up.

"Yah, that's true, man. Hey, you took sailing lessons with me last summer, right?" I nodded guiltily. "You see, I never forget a face. Never forget a name either — it's Patsy, right? No, Pammy. No wait, I know it's …"

"It's Peggy," I asserted, ending the familiar and slow torture.

"Oh yah, Penny." *Argh!* Well at least he didn't call me Piggy like my bratty little cousins did. "Well girl, don't just stand there. Go and get suited up and we'll see you back here in the pool." I skulked off, glad to be out of the spotlight.

Before we actually got in the pool Tornado gave us the rundown on what we would learn in the PADI diving course. We were going to learn safety procedures — like how to check all our gauges, how to get water out of our masks, buoyancy control, how to make a safe descent and ascent, and some emergency skills like sharing air with a dive partner. He said after two weeks in the pool we'd be ready for our first supervised open-water dive. That was the part I was most excited about.

"Okay, newbies, let's get in the pool and I'll go over proper buoyancy control and the four main points on your personal dive list — depth, air, time, and area. We call that your DATA. Some people write it on their hands so they don't forget. Me — I've got a mind like a steel trap — never forget a thing.... Right, Pammy? I mean Patty!" *Oh brother, what a doorknob!*

That first day I felt like a stuffed sausage in my wet suit, but it wasn't long before it started to feel more like a second skin. And with help from my flippers I loved the feeling of gliding up and down the length of the pool like a sleek black seal. There was no doubt about it, scuba diving was my thing and I was going to be even better at it than sailing.

The day Aunt Margaret and Uncle Stewart left on their cruise was bittersweet. It took no time at all for life at home without them to take on a predictable routine — school, diving lessons, then evenings of torture by Great Aunt Beatrix. Besides setting the table and reciting grace before every supper, I had to learn about the history of that stupid china that Duff broke.

"Did you know that the Chinese exported porcelains, such as this, to Europeans as far back as the 1600s?" asked Aunt Beatrix one evening just before suppertime. "It was held in such high esteem that the English word for it soon became china — for the place it originated."

"Fascinating.... Now can we eat?"

"Oh, pishposh. We'll eat in a few minutes. Now one special thing about our family's china — besides the fact that it came directly from China by traders

— is its pattern." She pointed to the dainty blue-on-white pattern. "This is cobalt blue and was very valuable. It was first used more than a thousand years ago. The other thing you'll want to notice is this small symbol on the bottom ... each artist had his own unique mark or sign. It was important for the good artisans to identify themselves. The really gifted ones were invited to the palace to make pottery for the emperor. Isn't that fascinating?"

"Mind-numbing.... Now can we eat?"

"Peggy, are you not hearing me? This very porcelain, which belonged to your great great great grandmother, is some of the oldest china in the country." I could tell by the way her face was turning red Aunt Beatrix was quickly becoming annoyed with me. If I ever wanted this lecture to end with supper I knew I had to at least pretend some interest.

"Wow! So if it's so rare and valuable why do they sell dishes just like it in the department store?" Aunt Beatrix gasped, like I'd said a four letter word.

"My dear, the only similarity between this porcelain and the tableware they sell in the stores is its pattern. This willow pattern — said to tell the sad story of two star-crossed lovers forbidden to love one another — has been copied over the centuries by many people." Then she held up one of Aunt Margaret's precious plates to the light on the kitchen ceiling. "For it to be truly fine china it must be translucent like this — you see?" I could see a clear shadow of her hand behind the plate. "This is the kind of china enjoyed by kings and queens,

Peggy. The dishes sold in stores today are nothing but cheap replicas."

Aunt Beatrix went on for another ten minutes, telling me how cobalt blue first came from Persia, that it was the kaolin clay found in China that gave porcelain its translucent quality, and that all the decorations were hand painted — which explained why there were small differences in each plate. She finally stopped after grinding in the fact that porcelain china made in the emperor's Imperial factory had a *nian hao* — a Chinese date mark — painted on the bottom. There were only a small number of painters who had this job, so their style could be recognized like individualized handwriting.

So it was — night after night it was either a history lesson or what Aunt Beatrix liked to call practical life lessons. Like learning to polish the silver, make fruit preserves, and knit. Once supper was over and the dishes washed and put away the rest of the evening was mine. That's when I read about diving, or the history of the Pacific fur trade, or underwater archaeology — things I really cared about. I especially enjoyed reading Captain Whittaker's diary.

In the back of my mind I was also trying to figure out when it would be the perfect moment to pop the question about going with Dr. Hunter to find the *Intrepid*. Timing for this was everything — which is why I had to make sure I had enough stored up brownie points. That's where Aunt Beatrix came in. I figured it was impossible for Mom not to have noticed how cooperative I was being with the cranky old history professor. After all, the agony of being her improvement project had to be worth something — something real big.

One night while I was studying my PADI diving manual Aunt Beatrix sat down across the table from me.

"I wish you took that kind of interest in your school work, Peggy. Maybe then you'd do better on your English tests," she prodded. I was about to object when I caught Mom's eye. She gave me the "let it go, Peggy" look.

"Aunt Beatrix, you do realize that the school year is nearly finished and the time for trying to get my teacher's approval has long passed." Mom shot me a look. *Okay, I'll be quiet ... but I'm right.*

"Aunt Bea, I'm just happy that she is so passionate about this course. I'm sure the skills she's learning will spill over into other aspects of her life." That was my signal — tonight I'd ask Mom about going on the research trip. I waited until it was time for bed.

"I know Aunt Beatrix can be frustrating, Peggy, but I think she really enjoys spending time with you. She says you remind her of when she was young," Mom said as I snuggled under my blankets.

"She was young?" I asked, trying to look shocked. Mom ignored the question.

"She grew up in a different time, Peggy. A time when girls had few choices and the main goal was finding a man to marry. Then after that it was all about being the best homemaker for your family or best hostess for your husband's business dinner parties. Who she became was partly due to the times she lived in."

"Maybe, but it wouldn't be so bad if she would just stop trying to make me into Suzy homemaker or the queen of etiquette. Doesn't she get it? Nobody cares about that stuff anymore."

"True, but maybe they should."

"Mom, are you serious? Who cares if you eat with your elbows on the table, or whether you reach across instead of asking for someone to 'please pass the salt and pepper?' And what's the big deal about writing thank-you notes — I mean who does that stuff anyway?"

"Peggy, having good manners is more than just knowing which fork to use, or saying please and thank you. Etiquette is really about treating others with respect. Sometimes the smallest word and gesture can go a long way in maintaining harmony in a relationship. And remember, the quality of one's life is best expressed in the small details. Those are the things that can set you apart."

"Humph," I grunted. "That sounds just like something Aunt Beatrix would say." Mom smiled. "Mom, did you mean what you said about how my interest in diving might spill over into other parts of my life?"

"Sure, every new skill and bit of knowledge all adds up to making us more well-rounded people. I can't say how diving is going to do that for you — it's not exactly a skill you can use every day, but you never know." I was just about to tell her about the *Intrepid* when Aunt Beatrix called from her room.

"Elizabeth, come here right away. This cat of Margaret's has spit up something disgusting on the floor."

"Sorry, Pegs. Let's talk more in the morning." Thanks to Aunt Beatrix and Duff, the magic moment was gone. Maybe tomorrow would be the day.

After Mom left the room I pulled out the captain's journal. I tried to imagine what the original one looked like. Maybe it was bound in black leather. And the pages musky from age and so fragile they almost fell apart in your fingers. I closed my eyes and pictured the captain sitting at his desk, writing by candlelight, the ship swaying and creaking, the wind gently whistling, and the muffled voices of sailors on deck.

November 10th, 1811

We are now five weeks into our voyage and there is a growing and palpable uneasiness aboard the ship. It seems on most occasions Mister Lockhart is at the centre of it. Early yesterday morning Cook's boy, Ellis, was caught pinching a penny's worth of tobacco out of Mr. Lockhart's pouch and I was forced to flog him. I detest brutality but it is my duty to keep strict discipline aboard the ship and to make it a warning to the others that stealing will not be tolerated. Had I not done it, I am sure Mister Lockhart would have snatched the whip from out of my hand and been happy to complete the task. He urged me menacingly to give the boy thirty lashes and cried out with disgust when I stopped at five. As unlikely as it sounds, I feel certain he was amused by the spectacle. I am even suspicious of why he left his pouch open on the table to begin with.

To cheer the mood I ordered the men be given an extra ration of salt beef and a shot of rum for supper. It did the job somewhat. Then Mister Foster, my assistant boatswain, suddenly hailed us all to come observe what at first appeared to be a large black wave in the distance. As the entity drew nearer it became clear it was a whale — one so massive that it nearly equaled the Intrepid in length and breadth. Indeed, when it came up side of us there was such a stir amongst the men I am sure the earlier events of the day were near forgotten.

Some of the men are skilled in harpooning and wanted to kill the great humped animal. I forbade them on the premise that such a catch would take too many days to process and would put us far behind our schedule. Secretly I had not the heart to destroy such a magnificent thing. In the moments after the creature breached the surface, time seemed to stand still. I had felt it gaze into my eyes — and the event moved me beyond words.

For hours we could hear its deep, haunting song across the sea as it trailed behind us. It went on into the night and I found myself drifting asleep to this strange lullaby of nature. When I woke hours later the whale's song had ceased. In my long career as captain I never felt such deep loneliness. I yearn as never before to be

*once again amongst kin and hearth. I believe with all
my heart this is to be my final voyage.*

Captain James Whittaker

CHAPTER FIVE

"Okay, kids, today is our last lesson in the pool. On Friday we'll be diving in open water. Then Saturday you'll have your dive test. If all goes well you'll be certified divers. Cool, eh?" Tornado gave us the thumbs-up sign. I got goose bumps at the thought of it. "But hey, before any of that, you need to know one more thing — how to buddy breathe. It's an important procedure that just might save your life one day. Who can tell me what the steps are to safe buddy breathing?" My hand shot up. I'd studied the manual the night before and knew all the steps by heart.

"Okay, Pammy, tell us what you know." I was getting used to being called something new every day and hardly even noticed it anymore.

"Step one is to signal to your buddy. If you're low on air do this." I placed my hand against my chest with my fingers curled under. "But if you're out of air this is the signal to use." I sliced my hand back and forth across my throat, the out-of-air signal. "Then you should tap your regulator with one finger — that tells your buddy that you want to buddy breathe."

"Very good, Patty. I can see you did your homework. You one of those smarty bookworms?"

Tornado sniggered. I rolled my eyes — if only he knew how far he was from the truth. "Okay, okay, just kiddin'. So once you've signaled your buddy — what then?"

"You should stay calm and let your buddy take three breaths and hand the regulator to you. Before you take a breath, press the purge button on the regulator to clear it before you inhale. Take three normal breaths and pass it back to your buddy. When you're both calm and breathing normally, signal your buddy that you're ready to go up to the surface." I paused for a moment trying to recall one more important point. "Oh yah, it's important not to hold your breath, just exhale slowly when you don't have the regulator."

"And why don't we hold our breath when ascending?" Tornado asked the group.

"I know, I know," pleaded TB.

"Okay, Geronimo — tell us," urged Tornado.

"Holding your breath while ascending can lead to an air embolism ... that's where you get air in your blood veins and you feel like your entire head, guts, and body is going to explode."

"Gory stuff, man, right on. But that's enough for now ... don't want to scare everyone." By the looks on some of the kids' faces I'd say it was too late to worry about that. Tornado turned to me.

"Okay, since you and your friend seem to know what you're doing you'll demo buddy breathing for the rest of the class." *Why not,* I thought. *I've got all the steps down pat, so it should be easy.* Tornado gave us the signal and we got into the deep end of the pool. We had on extra weights so we dropped down fast. TB signaled that he wanted to be the first to practice being out of air and to share my regulator and air tank. Everything went perfectly. Then it was my turn to pretend I was out of air — it would be easy, since I knew more about it than anyone else in the class. I removed my regulator from my mouth and let it go. It floated behind my head. Then I gave TB the out-of-air signal. He took three deep breaths and passed his regulator to me. So far, so good. Then I pushed the purge button and took in three deep breaths. Then I immediately exhaled.

Wait! I wasn't supposed to do that.

The second after I exhaled I realized what I'd done. It's funny how when your lungs are empty your brain goes blank too. I started grasping around for my own regulator but couldn't reach it. Then I grabbed at TB's regulator. He kept giving me the hand signal to wait while he took two more deep breaths.

When he finally passed it to me I shoved it over my mouth. That's when I made my second mistake — instead of purging the water from the regulator I immediately began to inhale. Instantly my lungs began filling with water instead of air and I started choking. Then I got completely disoriented. I couldn't even tell which way led to the surface of the pool. As I tore frantically at my weight belt I saw the look of panic in TB's eyes. That was the last thing I saw before everything went black.

* * *

I don't know how long it was before I regained consciousness, but when I did I was laying flat on my back at the side of the pool and staring up at Tornado. He was shouting in my ear to "wake up."

"I'm not deaf," I moaned weakly. Then I quickly turned to the side and hurled all over his leg.

"So that's the thanks I get for saving your life."

"Ah, sorry, Tornado. I, uh ..." Someone handed Tornado a wad of paper towel. I looked up to the other students and to TB. If I hadn't been feeling as crappy as a flat cow patty I'd have laughed at the look on their faces.

"Okay, you guys, everything is all right. Pammy's mistake makes for a good learning opportunity for everyone. She exhaled too quickly, leaving herself with no air in her lungs. Of course the worst mistake she made was panicking — something you'll want to make note of in case you're ever in a situation like this." *Great, now I'll always be remembered as the kid who lost it in diving school and nearly killed herself panicking.* "But don't be discouraged — the more you practice with this stuff, the more comfortable you'll get underwater. Just stick to the safety rules and procedures I've taught you and you'll be fine." Right then I heard a loud whining sound. "Okay, Patsy, the ambulance is here. The medics are going to have a look at you."

"No, I don't ..." I tried rolling to my side to get up, but flopped back down, exhausted. I didn't have the strength to resist. Soon I was prodded and checked over by two ambulance guys.

"Hey, that was pretty exciting," Tornado joked with one of them. "But that artificial resuscitation thing was tricky." I looked over at TB and groaned.

"TB, please tell me he didn't do mouth-to-mouth," I whispered. Just the thought of it made my stomach churn and I suddenly bent over and hurled again, this time on the medic's shoe. By the time they'd finished checking me out I was feeling a little better — physically anyway. The memory of it all was haunting me like a dream I couldn't wake up from. TB sat quietly by my side. He seemed to be in nearly as much shock as me. Besides nearly drowning, I now had a seriously disturbing image of Tornado giving me mouth-to-mouth resuscitation — it was like a barf stain on the brain.

"I called your house and let your great aunt know what happened," TB said.

"You called Aunt Beatrix! What'd you do that for?" I groaned while gripping my throbbing head.

"She sounded pretty calm, and said to tell you she's on her way."

"Thanks, TB," I said sarcastically. "Do you realize I'll never hear the end of this? Once Mom finds out what happened I can forget about the trip to find the *Intrepid*." I stood up to grab my towel and felt dizzy. TB caught my arm, but I pulled away. By the time I came out of the girls' change room he'd gone home and Aunt Beatrix was there waiting for me with a taxi. Strangely, I was sort of glad to see her. And even better, she hardly said a word the whole way back.

It happened to be one of Mom's late nights at work and Aunt Beatrix agreed not to tell her so she wouldn't worry and come racing home. Aunt Beatrix made chicken noodle soup and fresh cheese buns. I wasn't used to her being so quiet — or nice. Strangely, I found it annoying. To get her going I sat hunched, elbows on the table, slurping my soup. When that didn't get a rise out of her I pulled bits of my bun off and started feeding Duff on my lap. But she still didn't say anything.

Finally I couldn't take the silence any longer, so I said, "I'll bet you're just aching to say, 'It was a terrible way to learn a lesson, Peggy. Now you can see that diving lessons was a dumb idea.'"

But Aunt Beatrix didn't answer me, just sipped at her soup daintily.

"You probably think I should give it up," I continued. "Well, you can relax. I am giving it up."

Aunt Beatrix used her napkin to daub at her mouth and then rested her hands in her lap, posture perfect, manners impeccable. She cleared her throat, which was her signal that she was about to say something important.

"Peggy, my dear, you couldn't be more wrong. What happened today was just a small setback. I'm sure you'll get past this." I didn't expect that from her.

"Well, it doesn't matter because I'm done with it, okay?" Aunt Beatrix smiled and the intricate web of wrinkles at the corners of her eyes made her appear almost sweet.

"You say that now, but give it a day or so and I'm sure you'll see you can't give in to fear. When life knocks us down we just have to pick ourselves up and keep going."

I didn't have the strength to argue with her so I shuffled out of the kitchen and flopped down on the sofa to watch TV. I flicked through the channels looking for one of those mindless shows that don't require any intelligent thinking, hoping to keep my mind off the things I was too tired to think about.

Soon Mom came home and I could tell by the hushed voices in the kitchen that Aunt Beatrix was filling her in on the details. When she came into the living room I could see the concern on her face. She handed me a cup of my favourite mint hot chocolate topped with whipped cream. Then she snuggled in close and put her arms around me. Mom was my weak spot and knew exactly how to melt my hardened heart. I wiped angrily at the tears welling up in my eyes.

"I know what you're going to say, Mom. But my mind is made up. I suck at diving and I'm giving it up."

"Peggy, it must have been a really scary thing that happened to you today." That was an understatement if ever there was one. After a few minutes of silence, she continued. "If it was anyone else, I might say, sure, quit the diving lessons. But you're not a quitter, honey. You need to learn from today's experience and then go on to become the best diver...." Then she paused. "... And underwater archaeologist in the world." I burnt my lips on the hot chocolate when she said that. "Yes, I know about your plans, young lady. And by now you should know better than to try and keep secrets from your mother."

"But how —"

"The day after you signed up for diving lessons I got a call from Dr. Hunter. We had a nice conversation ... that is after I got over the shock. He told me about the expedition to find that sunken ship and how much you wanted to go along." I could feel my stomach start to heave and took three deep breaths to settle it back down. "Oh, and I also spoke to TB's mom and learned that the scuba lessons was all your idea — not TB's." My face suddenly flushed with heat and I wriggled nervously.

"I'm sorry I tricked you, Mom. It was a dumb ..."

"Don't get me wrong, at first I was fuming over your deceptiveness and I'm still working on what would be the best consequence to give you for lying to me. But I also realize archaeology is your life's passion, Peggy. And going on this expedition would be an amazing opportunity that will help you to reach your goal of becoming an archaeologist one day. Even Dr. McKay agreed this was an important opportunity not to be missed." Mom was pretty cool. While I was scheming about the right moment to ask her, she was waiting to drop her own little bomb. I leaned in to her heavily and kissed her cheek.

"Mom, I can still become an archaeologist. I just won't be the kind that excavates sunken ships or other underwater sites."

"So that's it? You're going to quit diving and let the opportunity of a lifetime go down the drain?" I couldn't bear the look of disappointment on her face.

"Mom, I'm really tired. I think I need to go to sleep. Maybe we could talk about this tomorrow."

"Okay, Peggy. But just remember this — sometimes life's best adventures start out like disasters. The thing is to not give up too easily and miss the surprise ending."

I stumbled up the stairs, glad to have my room back to hide out in. I flopped down on my bed, pulled the covers over my head and closed my eyes. I tried my best not to think, but it was no use. Besides reliving the images of nearly drowning over and over I kept thinking about what Mom said. Going with Dr. Hunter to find a sunken ship was definitely an adventure ... but was it supposed to be my adventure? I glanced over at the nightstand where I'd left Captain Whittaker's journal. I wondered if I'd find my answers there. I picked it up and leafed through the pages of scratchy cursive words and finally settled down to read.

November 21st, 1811

We entered St. Catherine's harbour this morning with our flag at half mast. We received a full gun salute from the fort and we returned in kind.

When we landed I ordered the men to obtain a few essentials and then dismissed them for the rest of the day. They need time to come to grips with the passing of young Albert Smedley and I can think of no better way than to give them shore leave so they can unwind from the snarls of these recent drastic events.

Herewith are the known details regarding Mr. Smedley's death:

On the evening of November 18th I was in my quarters. I heard an unusual amount of cheering and cavorting coming from the men. When I went to see what all the merriment was about I learned that poor Albert Smedley was competing against Mister Wilson in a race to the top of the main mast. The true test of a sailor is to climb the height of the tallest mast. Wilson is one of my most experienced crewmen, while Mister Smedley was one of my clerks and certainly had not fully developed the strength or skills for such a feat. Unfortunately they were already near the top, where Smedley was about to make the fatal mistake of securing himself to the pulley. It was then that a strong wind picked up and it became imperative that we trim the sails. I ordered the men to come down immediately, but by then the young Smedley was fully stuck with fear. Wilson was instructed to help him to disengage from the mast. As he struggled to follow orders the lad tumbled off, hit the foresail, and was flung into the sea. Alas, like most of my men Mister Smedley could not swim. We tried throwing him a rope, but it was futile for the waves engulfed him like a hungry dragon. I had such a menacing reaction to the poor boy's flailing and calls for help that my men had to hold me back from flinging myself into the water to save him. No good would have come of it, for I, too, cannot swim and would have simply joined him at the bottom of the sea. Since that night not one of us has slept easy.

I will report further on this tragic event when more details are learned.

Captain James Whittaker

Terrific, just what I needed to read after what I'd been through today. I threw the journal across the room. Just then Mom poked her head into my room.

"Peggy, TB's at the front door. He wants to talk to you." I rolled my head and sighed deeply. I didn't feel like talking or seeing anyone, much less TB. I'd been awful to him, but I didn't have the energy to explain myself right now.

"Tell him I've gone to bed." It wasn't a lie really.

"I think he's worried about you. Just come and say hello." I groaned.

"Mom, I just can't face him right now. Just tell him I'll call his cell phone."

"Hi TB," I said weakly a few minutes later. "What's up?"

"Nothin' much ... just wanted to see how you're doing. Are you still feeling sick? Hey, I'll bet the Tornado's leg will never be the same." He chuckled and I had to smile too. "What I mostly wanted to say was I was sorry for calling your aunt. I never thought what —"

"No, you don't need to feel sorry. I'm the one who should be sorry. Not only did I screw up our dive lesson, but I was pretty nasty when you were just trying to help. Friends?"

"Absolutely. So how did your mom take it? I sure would hate it if this got in the way of you going to find the *Intrepid*."

"Ah, well about that … yah, it looks like that's off."

"Really, your mom was that upset? Give her a couple of days and she'll —"

"TB, I gotta go. I'm still feeling kind of weak and want to go to bed. See you tomorrow, okay?" After I'd hung up I looked at the captain's journal on the floor where I'd chucked it and shuddered. Since I was already bound to have nightmares I decided to find out what happened next.

November 29th, 1811

The past several days were much occupied with the task of taking on fresh supplies and this kept us all from dwelling on the recent tragedy. Now that we are back at sea and nearing Cape Horn I am grateful the weather is on our side.

I have inquired with a few more of the men about what they know of the day of Mister Smedley's death. I am beginning to see the common thread that ties each of their stories together. It is clear from the start of this voyage there have been an inordinate number of disputes amongst the crew. Though they were mainly petty things, I already had an inkling that most of them originated in some way with Mister Lockhart. Now that I have heard from Mister Carver I am sure of it.

As mentioned, poor Smedley and Lockhart appeared to be friends, though it seems Mister Lockhart believed the boy to be weak and in need of muster. I learned that some of the men resented this friendship and taunted Smedley. The lad never complained to me about the matter, yet somehow I should have known. I am guilty of not seeing his agony and offering him guidance. The day of the drowning, Mister Lockhart offered up the boy as amusement for the men by betting that Smedley could best Mister Wilson in a mast race. As sometimes occurs when the work is done and the men idle, they enjoy some competition. They like to flex their strength in some test of skill. I do not usually interfere as it has always been done in good nature and with no harmful intent. The entire crew bet Wilson to win … I do not believe it was because they disliked the boy so intensely. They saw it as their opportunity to win back their wages lost to Lockhart while gambling. They knew with certainty that Mister Smedley was no match for the more experienced Mister Wilson. I cannot imagine what Lockhart was thinking, except perhaps he was trying to improve his standing with the crew, and young Smedley, who had become so eager to please the gentleman, allowed himself to be used in this way.

I find Mister Lockhart's lack of compassion despicable and I still cannot speak civilly to the man. The last time we dined together I nearly hurled my prized porcelain china at him. That would have been a tragedy *for it is part of a set presented to me by the Emperor on my last voyage to the Orient. For the time being I prefer to take my supper in my private quarters. This is better for me — and for the chinaware.*

I have ordered Mister Carver to keep a closer eye on Mister Lockhart and report back to me twice daily his interactions with the crew. He may be part owner along with my respected master, Mister Astor, but I am still captain of this vessel. Should the need arise I will be forced to confine him to his quarters until some arrangement can be made. In the meantime I have forbidden the men to play cards or gamble in any manner.

Captain James Whittaker

The next morning sunlight poured through my window. After the fogginess in my head cleared, the previous day's catastrophe crept back into my mind like a nasty little spider. I knew Mom was downstairs waiting to know what I'd decided to do about the scuba diving. If I told her what I was thinking she'd feel like I let her down — worse, that I'd wasted her hard earned money — and she'd be right. Instead of facing her I whipped on some clothes, grabbed my school bag, and snuck out the front door before she even knew I was awake.

When I was halfway to school the most annoying thing happened. Aunt Beatrix's words stomped around in my head: "… it's your moment-by-moment conduct that will determine the success of your life ... be honest, temperate, polite, clean, and face up to your problems with courage ... take care in even the small things and you'll find when the going gets tough you'll be able to stay the course."

For the rest of the day I tried to push my great aunt and her advice out of my mind, but it was stuck in there like old gum on the bottom of my shoe. The other annoying thing was TB plastering me with questions. "When you nearly drowned did you see a white light, Peggy? How about angels and a pearly gate?"

"Can't talk right now, TB. Gotta get home," I told him as I dashed away on my bike after the dismissal bell. "Catch you later."

Instead of going home though, I rode down to Blackie's Spit and found myself a log to sit on. As the waves lapped rhythmically onto the beach I sat and formulated my reasons for dropping out of scuba diving. When I had my speech worked out I rode my bike home. The closer I got the more I realized that my excuses were lame and Aunt Beatrix would see through them in a moment. I also knew that she'd remind me of the sacrifice Mom made so I could take the lessons. Then Mom would point out how disappointed Eddy and Dr. Hunter would be. And if that wasn't bad enough, there was a niggling little question in my mind about what Captain Whittaker would think I should do.

When I got in the house I tried to sneak up to my room, but Aunt Beatrix's hearing was sharper than I thought.

"So there you are. I hope you're finally over yesterday's little mistake and ready to have another go at this diving business."

"A little mistake — I nearly drowned! It was a good thing I was in the pool when it happened. If I'd been in open water you could actually be talking to a ghost right now." Aunt Beatrix started to *tsk* at me. I could feel the blood rushing to my face.

"Oh pishposh! You're Peggy Henderson, of the stock of Reynolds ... and Reynoldses are not quitters."

I sighed and flopped down on the sofa. That's when I knew there was no point in trying to refuse — that's because I'd never get a moment's worth of peace if I didn't give it one more try.

"All right — I'll try again. But be warned ... if I drown this time, you'll have no one to blame but yourself."

That night just before I went to sleep, Mom came and sat on the side of my bed. "I'm really glad you decided to stick with it, Peggy. I'm proud of you." She kissed the top of my head. While she might have been proud, I felt like I was being forced to dive into a pool of sharks. "Hey, by the way — they announced on the news tonight that 'some underwater archaeologists' were off to find the long lost *Intrepid*." I sat up straight. "They said it would be the biggest discovery of its kind and likely mean big bucks for the researchers too. I could only think how exciting it was that my daughter was going to be one of those people to find it."

What? How did the media find out? Dr. Hunter said if this got out to the media prematurely treasure hunters would get in there and alter the site — it could ruin everything. I just hoped he didn't think it was me who blabbed the news. I shrank back down in my bed and spent the next several hours in and out of sleep.

Friday afternoon came too soon. Even though I knew the scuba diving manual inside and out, I wasn't a bit sure of how I'd do in open water. When Mom talked to Tornado on the phone he called it a minor glitch. He said: "Could happen to any beginner. Tell that Patty Cake she's a natural at this stuff and to just get back up on her donkey and ride."

Mom smiled. "Does he talk like that all the time?"

"Like that or worse!" He might call my near-drowning a minor glitch, but he wasn't the one who was panicking at the bottom of the pool. Just then I realized something — if I failed my PADI test it would all be over. I wouldn't have to listen to Aunt Beatrix or Mom telling me to get back out there. I wouldn't have to feel guilty about letting Eddy or Dr. Hunter down either. Failing would be my way out.

TB came by the house and we walked together to meet Tornado and the class at the pier near Blackie's Spit.

"I'm glad you made it, Peggy. Today's going to be so awesome — an actual dive in open water. Hey, wouldn't it be cool if we found an old sunken ship filled with long lost treasure?" I punched his arm.

"If there was a sunken ship out there don't you think the thousand or so other people who've been diving and snorkeling around Blackie's Spit all these years might have seen it by now?"

"As I see it, anything's possible. If a dipstick kid like you gets a chance to go looking for some long lost ship off the coast of B.C. with a bunch of scientists, then it's possible I'll find treasure today." He shot me back a punch in the arm and sped off towards the pier before I could catch him.

"So you're back," Tornado said when I arrived at the pier out of breath. "I didn't really think you'd be here today." That was annoying — I hated that he assumed I'd be a coward.

"Yup, I'm here … ready to get back up on my high horse." I thought he'd appreciate the old metaphor.

"Are you sure you're okay, kid? 'Cause we're all here for diving lessons, not horseback riding. Maybe you should get checked out." Some of the other kids giggled. "Just pulling your arm, Pegsy. I know that saying too … kind of like: 'If at first you don't succeed try, try again.' Right?" Imagine that — he finally got one right.

"Okay kiddos, today is the day you've all been waiting for," Tornado announced when everyone finally arrived. Not exactly true in my case. "After we get suited up we're all going to go through an equipment check. Then we'll review emergency procedures — Patty girl here is going to take us through that part …" My face felt like it was going to melt right off my skull. "So let's get started."

When everyone was ready I reviewed all the procedures from the manual. Then Tornado gave everyone further safety instructions. Just as TB and I were about to walk with everyone else down to the end of the pier Tornado stopped us.

"Hold on, you two. Now I know TB here is breathless over the thought of being your partner ..." He chuckled at his lame joke, while I willed my cheeks from turning crimson red. "... But for your first open water dive I'll be going down with you both. Just want to make sure there's no more of that mouth-to-mouth resuscitation business ..." Gross — my sentiments exactly. I felt like a dolt that Tornado had to accompany us. But the sooner he could see that I was no good at diving — the sooner the test would be over.

After we got in the water Tornado said: "Okay, kiddo, we're going to try the buddy breathing again and we're going to keep doing it until you either swallow a fish tank of seawater or get it right." *Could he be more insulting?*

"I'll give it another try. I just hope I don't choke up with fear."

"Don't worry, we've got your back," TB said. Tornado nodded.

As we bounced around on the waves I could feel my heart pounding inside me. A part of me wanted to be the coward Tornado expected me to be, but there was another part of me who was trying to recall all the things Mom and Aunt Beatrix had said to give me courage.

"Just remember to breathe calmly as we descend. And remember this is going to be fun!" TB said.

"That's right!" Tornado smacked my back and I caught a mouthful of salt water. "Okay, let's go."

Even though it went against every instinct in my body I put my head under water and took my first tentative breaths through the regulator. Then I could hear it — scush-shhhh, scush-shhh, scush-shhh — it was the sound of my breathing under water. I looked over at Tornado, who was giving me the okay sign. I returned the signal. Then he gave me the signal it was time to descend. My heartbeat went into hyper speed, but I knew better than to hold my breath. *Easy, steady breaths,* I told myself over and over again. And down we went….

December 25th, 1811

It was a pleasant Christmas Day for the men. The general merriment included carol singing, rum cake, and for dinner a fine cooked turkey — we had been nursing the tasty fellow along since St. Catherine's for this very purpose. Afterwards the men partook in games of various sorts and more carol singing.

The air is getting warmer as we near the Sandwich Islands. According to my first mate, rations are getting low, so we will wood and water there and may stay on for some time. I know the men look forward to it and it will be a welcome respite for us all.

I am pleased to report that Mister Lockhart has been contrite of late and we have begun to take our supper together once again. Now that we know we will soon arrive at the Sandwich Islands our conversation is mostly about what to expect when we get there. No doubt the gentleman will want to exchange wares once we arrive so I am preparing him by sharing my experiences dealing with the aboriginal peoples of Hawai'i, particularly their customs. I daresay Mister Lockhart may be very knowledgeable in his dealings with the typical New York businessman. However, it is a completely different matter when one is standing as a stranger on the shore of a new people. Decorum and humility is of paramount necessity in such cases.

With the new year about to begin my hopes are high that things have finally settled and smooth sailing lies ahead with Mister Lockhart.

Captain James Whittaker

CHAPTER SIX

"Peggy, make sure you're careful and wear your life jacket at all times, okay? And it's important that you listen to Dr. Hunter." Mom crushed me in her arms like I was a memory-foam doll. Before she could say another word or change her mind about letting me go, I pecked her on the cheek and wriggled out of her arms. Grabbing my backpack, I turned to Eddy.

"C'mon, Eddy, we'd better get moving." I was glad she'd volunteered to drive me to Steveston docks to meet with Dr. Hunter instead of Mom. For one thing it guaranteed I'd be on time, and it also meant I could avoid all of Mom's last minute advice and mushing over me. Just when I thought I'd made a clean getaway, Aunt Beatrix piped up.

"Now remember, dear — put your best foot forward, display impeccable manners, remember that honesty is always the best policy, pull your own weight, be responsible, and for heaven's sake comb your hair." Aunt Beatrix stood next to Mom wagging her finger at me.

"Yes, Aunt Beatrix," I groaned. "Now that it's just the two of you maybe you should teach Mom a thing or two about china and how to make a good impression on her boss." She smiled like I'd just given her a great idea. Mom pursed her lips and narrowed her eyes. *Gotcha, Mom!*

When Eddy's rattling old truck finally turned the corner and we were heading up Crescent Beach road I sighed and opened the brown paper bag Aunt Beatrix had given me as I got in the truck. A warm, sweet smell filled the cab.

"Mmmm," I sighed. "I won't miss being Aunt Beatrix's improvement project, or all her lessons about old Chinese porcelain, but I will miss her baking and cooking." I handed Eddy a fresh carrot-and-chocolate-chip muffin still warm from the oven.

As we drove in silence I recalled the day I passed my diving test. Like the carrot muffin fresh from the oven, the memory of it warmed me all over. That night at dinner I couldn't stop talking. My fingers and toes were shriveled like prunes and my eyes still stung from the salt water that had seeped into my mask. But I was ecstatic, overjoyed, and even out-of-my-mind happy. I also knew that there was no way I was going to miss the chance to go looking for the *Intrepid*.

"How did you get so much water in your mask in the first place?" asked Mom. I could feel the rumble of joy deep inside me and wished I could explain better what it was like.

"I couldn't stop laughing, that's why. I wished you'd been there, Mom. The moment we started to descend I felt like I'd been dumped into an aquarium."

"So what happened to being afraid?"

"That's the thing — it just vanished the moment I went under the water and saw all the sea life. It was like I had entered another world and it made me forget about being afraid." I rambled on about the seaweed that swayed like little green hula dancers, the crabs creeping about on the ocean floor, clams, catfish, the schools of tiny fish, and how beautiful and serene everything was. Even Aunt Beatrix couldn't get a word in edgewise. "And all the skills I learned in the pool somehow became second nature to me. I even passed buddy breathing with flying colours." When I closed my eyes I could see the fish and shells and dark-green water pierced by the shafts of sunlight. It felt so good when Mom told me how proud she was that I'd overcome my fear. Come to think of it, I was proud of myself, too.

"Glad to see you packed light, Peggy. There won't be much room on the boat." Eddy's voice broke me out of my reverie.

"That's what Dr. Hunter told me too. Now if I was one of those prissy girls Aunt Beatrix wanted me to be I'd have enough clothes, cosmetics, and hair product to sink a ship."

"Maybe you're wrong about your great aunt. Maybe she doesn't want you to be like that at all. Didn't you say she was the one who encouraged you to go back and finish the diver's training?"

"More like she hounded me," I mumbled with a mouth full of muffin. "She's doesn't believe in quitting, that's for sure."

"That sounds like a good aspiration," Eddy added. I wanted to change the subject, so I pulled out Captain Whittaker's diary.

"How's that going?" Eddy asked.

"This? Great. It's been kind of weird reading his thoughts about things as they were happening two hundred years ago. I get the feeling he was a good guy, but pretty formal. I bet he was someone that Aunt Beatrix would approve of. Do you want me to read a little to you?" I asked.

"That would be great. Go for it." As we sped along Highway 99 I opened the journal and began to slowly read the captain's scratchy writing. As the words left the page and filled the air I got goose bumps as it dawned on me that I was going into the watery grave of the man who wrote them.

January 9th, 1812

Yesterday we arrived at Hawai'i. It is the largest of the Sandwich Islands. The locals call it the Big Island. This marks my fifth — and likely final — voyage to the place. Each time upon arrival I feel melancholy for it reminds me of my dear friend and mentor, Captain James Cook. He named these the Sandwich Islands after my uncle, the Earl of Sandwich, some thirty-five years ago. I was just a boy of sixteen when I joined him on that first voyage to these islands. They were good days as I recall. Many years later Captain Cook returned here. At that time there was a dispute between him and the native Hawai'ians that brought a violent end to his great life. It still haunts me to this day. Nevertheless, as the captain said himself, "these are kind and welcoming people." I am grateful to be on good terms with King Kamehameha. He is a fearsome man and I have urged Mister Lockhart to take great care when negotiating with him.

Speaking of Mister Lockhart, it was most amusing to observe his great displeasure at the time of our arrival at Big Island. Once we dropped anchor in the bay some twenty of the handsomest youths swam out to greet us. Their persons were entirely naked. Then came their old men and women in canoes bearing heaps of fresh fruit and dried fish. I have been witness to such greetings in the past and in good form the crew responded to this welcome by handing out some trinkets such as glass beads, a few brass buttons, and some iron nails crafted by our blacksmith, Mister Hughes. Nothing too much, just tokens really.

Nevertheless, when Mister Lockhart saw this expression of generosity he called for an immediate cessation. In his own words, he said, "How in the name of God am I to drive negotiations with these savages if you give away the very items I intend to barter?" Since the agreement with Mister Astor was that I captain the ship and let Mister Lockhart head up the trading, I urged the crew to obey. Needless to say, I did inform Mister Lockhart later that such small gift giving is expected by most natives we have encountered. It is a small gesture that can set the mood for peaceful and friendly trading.

The young gentleman has much to learn. I only hope he heeds my warning when we meet with King Kamehameha tomorrow. The man is a pagan with dozens of wives and heaven knows how many children.

Nonetheless, he commands great respect and must always think he has the upper hand in negotiations.

The men have been in very high spirits since our arrival and are urging that we remain until the worst of the winter winds blow themselves out. Daily life aboard the ship offers too few hours of carefree distraction from swabbing, helming, and pushing a capstan. This is why a break on Big Island is a most pleasant place to unwind from the snarls of sea life. And after the added tension and complications we have endured it might be the best medicine. I shall have word with Mister Lockhart about the matter. Perhaps the congeniality of the island people will have a positive effect on him too.

Note to self: Tell Cook while we are in port no more salt beef or pork — the men need fresh meat to keep the scurvy at bay. I want them well refreshed and healthy for the long journey ahead.

Captain James Whittaker

"This Lockhart sounds like a real character," Eddy said. "Too bad we don't have time to read more … but there's Philip waiting. I wonder who that young woman is with him." As we got closer I realized the girl's face was familiar. Where had I seen her before?

"Hey, I know. She was our guide at the Maritime Museum. Her name is —"

"Amanda Marsh," Eddy jumped in once we were closer. "She was a student in my Archaeology Resource Management class a few years ago. Bright, eager … a lot like you."

"She's an archaeologist?"

"Yes, a maritime archaeologist and she's working on her Master's Degree — specializing in shipwrecks. You'll be in good hands with her, Peggy." I had a renewed sense of excitement when Eddy pulled up to the peer. Dr. Hunter and Amanda walked over to greet us.

"Well, hello there," Amanda sang out. "I can't believe it! Philip, this is the girl I mentioned a while ago, the one who came to the museum with her class. I told you I'd never met a more eager student." There it went again … my face melting into ten shades of red.

"Well, at least you remembered me for something good. My mom and aunts are always afraid I'll make my mark for all the wrong reasons." Everyone seemed to find that amusing and suddenly the last little bit of worry dissolved. "Talk about weird though … I never thought I'd be seeing you again, Amanda."

Dr. Hunter smiled. "One thing you'll discover soon, Peggy … the world of underwater archaeology is very small," he said. "In some ways that's a good thing and sometimes not so much. It must have been someone in the field who let the word slip out to the media that we were off to find the *Intrepid*." I could feel my face flush with panic.

"Well just in case you were thinking it was me, I promised you that even torture wouldn't make me talk and I meant it."

"I believe you, Peggy. But someone broke their promise. Now that it's out we've got to get moving before some guy with a camera shows up and starts asking a lot of questions." Amanda grabbed my pack and pointed to the boat.

"Follow me, Peggy, it's time we board the *Sea Weed*." I gave Eddy a hug, waved goodbye, and quickly followed after Amanda. I only got a quick glance of the boat before we bound up the gangway. It seemed pretty big … not like a ship or anything, but it was probably fifty or sixty feet long. It had two tall metal poles sticking out from each side with cables strung along them.

"Is this a fishing boat?" I asked.

"Yes, it's a trawler. But it's not used for fishing anymore — not since the archaeology department picked it up a few years ago for a good price." On the deck of the boat I noticed there were winches, pulleys, and cables from the days it was used for fishing.

"Is that a fish net?" I asked, pointing to a pile of rope tucked under a tarp.

"You're a curious kind of a kid, aren't you? After that day at the museum, I shouldn't be surprised. But I sure didn't expect you'd actually take my advice and learn to scuba dive. You won't regret it — I can promise you that. I've banked more than seventy dives now, and I still never get tired of going to the ocean floor — particularly when diving around sunken ships." I knew Amanda and I were soon going to be good friends.

A few minutes later we were waving goodbye to Eddy on shore as our boat slowly pushed off. I felt a tingle all over as I watched her get smaller and smaller. Everything was perfect: fresh salt air, seagulls soaring overhead and squawking, the sun glinting across the calm ocean surface — and me, Peggy Henderson, off to find a sunken ship. I sighed, sure it would be easy sailing ahead.

When Steveston was nothing but a sliver on the horizon Amanda took me around and introduced me to the rest of the crew. Scott Robinson and Marnie Redfield were both marine archaeologists and worked with Amanda at the Maritime Museum.

"Hey, nice to meet you, Peggy," Marnie said warmly. Scott gave me a high-five while he read out coordinates to Marnie. We then went to the bridge to meet Dr. Hernando Sanchez. Like Dr. Hunter, he was a professor at a university and was visiting from Mexico City. He didn't look like anyone from Mexico that I'd ever met before — his hair was flat on his skull like he'd greased it into place, and his front teeth were rimmed with gold fillings.

"I am sure you are a good 'leedle' girl, but I told Dr. Hunter it is a terrible mistake to bring a child on such an important research trip," said Dr. Sanchez. He spoke with a heavy accent, and when he said the word "little," it sounded like "leedle." My cheeks burned and I felt silly standing there with my outstretched hand as it became obvious he wasn't going to shake it. "You stay out of the way leedle girl and whatever you do — don't touch the equipment, especially the radio. And remember, this is no kids' day camp!"

Jerk — I might be a kid, but I wasn't a two-year-old.

"Now Hernando … be nice," said Dr. Hunter in a chuckle that sounded a lot like my mom's when she was trying to divert an argument between Aunt Margaret and me. "Peggy comes highly recommended by one of my oldest colleagues and a good friend. I'm sure she's going to be a big help to us." He patted my shoulder, while giving Amanda a nod. "Maybe Peggy should check out the rest of the boat." Amanda urged me to follow her.

"Never mind Sanchez … he's a bit of a control freak and has no sense of humour. Just do your best to stay clear of him, okay." I nodded. "Good. It's time you get a tour of the boat and see where we store our safety equipment." I must have looked a little surprised. "Nothing to be alarmed about — Captain Hunter expects everyone aboard to be well informed and know what to do in the unlikely event of an emergency." She sounded like one of those flight attendants who try to explain safety procedures to passengers too busy breaking out their snacks and new magazines. While I hardly ever payed attention either, I made sure to listen to what Amanda was saying.

"Why do you call Dr. Hunter the captain?" I asked as I followed her down the steep set of stairs into a cramped hallway.

"When we're out on the water everyone calls him that. He's in charge of the boat and of the expedition so it just seems fitting to call him Captain." We walked down the narrow hallway, past the noisy engine room, a lab, and some private quarters. Finally we came to what looked like a dining area.

"Here's the galley where we prepare and eat our meals. You'll be expected to help out … just wanted you to know in case you thought you were on one of those fancy cruise ships with endless buffet meals." She smiled.

Next, we came to some cupboards with shiny brass latches. "We keep all the life vests, the life raft, supplies, flares, and so forth in here. Captain Hunter expects everyone to know procedures and how to use the equipment. He's been known to give surprise emergency drills so we all have to be ready."

"What time are these drills?"

"Just like you'll never know when a real emergency arises, neither do we know when the captain will call for a drill … so like a good scout, 'be prepared.'" Amanda handed me a small craft safety manual. "Study this later. Captain Hunter is very serious about safety and expects you to know it by bedtime — just like the rest of the crew." I must have looked worried. "Don't freak out, and don't hesitate to ask questions if you're unclear about something." It hadn't gone unnoticed that Amanda said the word "crew" as though I were one of them. That's when I realized that besides Dr. Sanchez, everyone else was expecting me to pull my own weight. I secretly promised right there that I wouldn't let them down. And I was going to prove to Dr. Sanchez that I wasn't some "leedle" kid tagging along who needed babysitting.

"Here's where you and I will sleep." Amanda pointed to two small bunks hanging off the wall. "And down there is the head. It's finicky so make sure you never flush anything down besides the natural stuff and never pull the chain more than once."

"Why? Will this place turn into a poop deck?" I snickered at my witty boat joke.

"Ha ha ha. As a matter of fact it could. And if you think Dr. Sanchez is grouchy now, wait until you find out what he's like if he doesn't get his morning potty time!" I squirmed — now that was a seriously gross image.

"Why is it called the head anyways?" I asked to change the subject ... slightly. "Kind of silly when they could just call it a toilet."

"That term came before the days of toilets. In the old days sailing ships had a tiny platform at the bow for sailors to use as a makeshift outhouse. By being in the very front of the ship, the area naturally became cleaned by splashing waves, and since the wind came from behind, it kept odours away from the rest of the crew. The bow also happened to be where they always fastened the figurehead of a beautiful woman or a bronze eagle or something. So if a sailor needed to relieve himself he would say he was going to the head of the ship." Amanda had a way of making even the history of crapping sound interesting. Definitely some trivia TB would want to know when I got home.

"I'm going on deck to check in with the captain. So why don't you settle yourself in and come on up when you're ready." After Amanda left I crawled up onto my bunk and unpacked my clothes, placing them into a small compartment above. I felt like I was in a cozy little cave, being gently rocked by the waves. It must be how a baby in a cradle feels. Soon the rocking made me a little tired. I decided I'd lie down and read some of Captain Whittaker's journal — just for a few minutes.

February 27th, 1812

All is ruined!

Yesterday, while I was afoot in the village making arrangements for the grand dinner party in honour of King Kamehameha, I foolishly left Mister Lockhart aboard. The king arrived early and asked for a tour of the ship. When they came to the weapons room Mister Lockhart rudely refused our guest access, telling him "coloureds" are never permitted in our weapons storehouse. As told to me by my first mate, Mister Carver, the king was enraged — his face red with anger over Mister Lockhart's comments. Thereafter he hastily left the ship.

Typically it is my rule to never encourage aboriginals to board the ship in the event that their motives prove to be hostile. But on this occasion the king was guest of honour, so to refuse his request was not only foolish, but lacking manners. Had I been aboard this never would have happened.

With Mister Lockhart's previous failures in decorum we were already on shaky ground with the king.

Indeed, the dinner aboard the Intrepid *was intended to mend this rupture in our standing.*

The moment I returned to the ship I knew something was amiss from the wide-eyed stares of the men. When I was told the story I immediately sent out a messenger, but he was met at Kamehameha's fortress by angry guards. When he came back visibly shaken I knew then that relations with the king had been severed.

After the murder of my dear friend, Captain James Cook and his crew, I knew full well the potential danger with which we were faced. I ordered the men to be on the ready and to prepare for departure. After we had become enemies of King Kamehameha, I was sure that none of the chiefs from surrounding islands would do business with the Intrepid.

Clearly we had no choice but to leave. Miserably, Mister Smythe, our assistant blacksmith, and two other crewmen, Mister Archiebald and Mister Lloyd had not yet returned from the east side of Big Island where they were exploring for usable minerals. I waited for them for as long as I felt was reasonably safe. If things had been different I would have sent forces to bring them back, but the longer we lingered the greater the risk to the rest of the crew and to the ship.

When Kamehameha's men started gathering by the hundreds on the shore I decided there was nothing further to be done and ordered that we pull up anchor and set sail. The best I can hope for now is that future relationships with Mister Astor's fleet are not jeopardized and that the three crewmen left behind will go unharmed. My men were horrified that I left without

Smythe and the others, but none will have to bear the guilt with which I am now burdened. I vow that on our return to New York I will find the first ship departing for the Sandwich Islands and instruct them to search for my men. I pray they remain safe until then.

We are secure in our food source. The cattle which we brought from St. Catherine's were in good circumstances, having been well refreshed on shore, and we were successful in procuring a good supply of grass for them. Nevertheless, I am worried about the men's reaction and I fear we are in for an especially difficult stretch. They know to whom they can thank for this abrupt departure from paradise and the abandonment of their friends. I fear there may be some retaliation. For a time I will need to keep close eye on the crew, and keep Mister Lockhart close at hand so that no harm comes to him.

Captain James Whittaker

"Okay, Peggy, what needs to happen should we discover there is a leak?" asked Dr. Hunter as the crew sat around the galley that evening. I knew it was important to make a good impression, so I had to get this right.

"Okay, once the deck hatches are opened, a crew member starts the bilge pump, while another gets out the extra buckets. The engine is not to be shut off, unless the leak is from the engine hoses." The captain kept a steady gaze on me that made me a little nervous.

"What if it's not a leak? What if there's an explosion or fire?"

"Right, well then all crew needs to be ready to go overboard ... with a life jacket. If possible use fire extinguishers. If not, cut off air to the area. If that doesn't bring the fire under immediate control, someone should be on the radio calling out MAYDAY, MAYDAY, MAYDAY!" I shouted, forgetting this wasn't a real drill. "Use flares if help is in sight, gather all flotation devices available, and prepare to abandon ship."

"Good. What if the emergency is a man overboard?" Dr. Hunter continued testing.

"MAN OVERBOARD, MAN OVERBOARD," I shouted. "You keep shouting that until the skipper cuts the engine, all the while you never take your eye off the person in the water. When you can, throw a life ring or seat cushion to him. Whatever you do, don't jump into the water to assist. That could mean two drowned crew members." I suddenly realized those last words were written by Captain Whittaker in his log as he watched poor Albert Smedley drowning. The memory of it oozed back into my mind like soggy mud and made me shudder. I was glad that I was a strong swimmer.

"Good work, Peggy. Now I can see why Edwina has so much faith in you. You're a bright young lady." I squirmed as the rest of the crew applauded — well, everyone except Dr. Sanchez. "Okay, it's getting late. We're going to let down anchor and catch a few hours of sleep." I glanced out the porthole and was glad to see the town of Powell River nearby.

"Dr. Hunter ... I mean Captain Hunter ... it's only eight thirty. I'm a kid, and even I never go to bed this early."

"By the time we secure the boat, update our location with the Coast Guard, and tuck ourselves in it will be nine p.m. We're up again at three thirty so we can get an early start before the wind and waves pick up."

Up at 3:30 a.m.? What was the point of going to sleep at all?

Soon enough everyone aboard was fast asleep ... everyone except me. I had all the ingredients for a good sleep ... cozy berth, gentle waves, my favourite pillow from home ... and I'd had a long and exciting day. But all the same I couldn't sleep a wink. I reasoned it must have been because of the nap I'd had earlier in the day after reading Captain Whittaker's journal. I tossed for a while longer hoping that I'd eventually nod off, but soon I knew it was futile. I had the top bunk so when I quietly rolled out of bed I did my best not to rest my feet on Amanda's bunk. I sighed with relief when I heard her snoring softly. Then I made my way down the narrow hall, passed the engine room, which was eerily quiet, and on to the galley. I flicked on the small lamp that set off a warm glow in the tiny room. I noticed for the first time a small bookshelf above the porthole. On it was a neat row of books. I scanned the titles: *Essays in Maritime Archaeology; Techniques for*

Identifying Trade Beads; Historic Relations Between European Traders and First Nations of the Northwest; and *Methods for Preserving Artifacts Removed From a Saltwater Environment.* They were all titles that would put your typical kid to sleep — but not me. I was about to reach for the book on preserving artifacts when I noticed another neat row of books — novels with covers worn from years of use. Maybe this is where I'd find myself a nice bedtime story. I scanned the titles: *The Rhyme of the Ancient Mariner; The Ghost Pirates; The Flying Dutchman; Curse of the Black Pearl; Pirates of the Caribbean.* Not exactly the kind of stories that sweet dreams were made of, but maybe I could at least tire myself out with one of them. I pulled down *Treasure Island* by Robert Louis Stevenson. I'd never read it, but I remembered Uncle Stewart saying it was one of his favourite books when he was my age.

From the moment I cracked open the dry old pages on that leather bound book I was hooked. *Treasure Island* was not one of those stories you start and then put down easily. The kid, Jim, seemed to be close to getting his throat slit, like, five times in the first three chapters. What was the matter with this guy ... he should have known from the moment that the old pirate showed up at his father's inn that trouble was close behind. Just when things were getting really tense I heard a noise coming from outside the boat — like water splashing. It gave me a creepy feeling, especially since I was alone. Well, I wasn't actually alone, but with everyone asleep it sure felt that way. I knew I was a little jumpy just because my imagination was already in high gear. I'd just come to the end of the scene where Jim and his mom heard the pirates ransacking the inn in search of the treasure map and were hiding under the bridge. I was about to start the next chapter when I heard the splashing noise again. My heart skipped a beat and then started to race. I got up on my knees and glanced out the window but could see nothing but thick fog. Not even the night lights of Powell River were visible any more. As I sat, ears pricked, I heard the sound of water splashing a third time — it was coming from the aft of the boat. One side of my brain told me to hide, or at the very least get back in my bed. The other urged me to find out what it was. Before I had time to change my mind, I jumped off the seat and went through the galley towards the back, climbed the stairs and came out on the deck that led to the helm where Captain Hunter steered the boat. As I stood in the black silence, I heard the lapping of the waves on the boat, and felt the cool air tickle the hairs on my arms. The silence and the fog were like backdrops to some scary movie and I couldn't shake the images of throat-slitting pirates hauling themselves up over the sides of the boat.

"You're nuts, Peggy Henderson," I said aloud for reassurance. Just then a swift dark figure surfaced from the water and just as quickly sank down again with a little splash that left the boat rocking. I didn't know what it was and didn't stick around to find out. I ducked back inside the cabin as fast as I could, dropped the book off on the table as I passed through the galley, painfully stubbed my toe on the bench, and finally stumbled back to my cabin out of breath. When I finally found the ladder I grabbed onto it and hauled myself up to my bunk. I panted as quietly as I could, trying to catch my breath and hoping Amanda didn't hear me.

"You didn't flush any toilet paper, right?" Amanda's sleepy voice came from below. "Remember, only the natural stuff."

"Right, nothing but the real thing," I answered back, glad to hear her voice even though I'd tried my best not to wake her.

"Good. See you in a couple of hours," Amanda whispered up to me.

I don't know how long it took, but I obviously fell asleep. The next thing I knew the engine was squealing and I could feel the boat was cutting through water. There was also a hint of light seeping through the porthole and the sound of clanging pots coming from the galley.

"Well, you're still alive then," said Amanda, smiling. "I didn't know if you were ever going to wake up." I looked at the clock. It read 5:30 a.m.

"Sorry, I didn't hear the wake up call," I mumbled.

"Don't worry, most people have the same experience the first night or two. It takes getting used to, sleeping on a boat. Good thing for you it's almost breakfast. You like pancakes and bacon?"

"Who doesn't?" I chirped.

* * *

All that day we sailed up the Inside Passage. We saw an eagle diving down and snatching up a fish at the last moment, caught a glimpse of a couple of killer whales — just their flukes and tail fins really, and had a pod of porpoises chasing the boat for about a half hour. I took comfort watching their sleek bodies leap effortlessly out of the water and felt sure it must have been a porpoise I'd seen and heard the night before. When he took breaks from steering the boat, Captain Hunter told me more about what we'd be doing when we arrived at the site.

"Once we've located the ship we'll create a point of reference — perhaps the anchor — that will allow us to find her again in the future. On our first dive we'll set up a grid system and take some photographs. We have to be really careful not to disturb anything. The ship and the artifacts that may be down there are in a state of equilibrium with the environment. If we suddenly upset that balance it could cause things to rapidly deteriorate."

"How do you plan to get the *Intrepid* out of the water?" I had never been part of an excavation this big before — maybe they'd bring in a bunch of heli- copters for an airlift or a ship with a crane.

"I'm not sure yet if we can even raise her off of the seafloor, Peggy. Sometimes the best thing to be done is to leave a sunken ship where it is. We'll have to wait and see. For certain, we're going to do our best to minimize any threats to it now that news of its existence has gotten out to the public. We want to establish this as a protected site, then divers who are mutually interested in preserving the *Intrepid* will help us protect her — they'll be like our eyes and ears — watching out for danger."

"Do you think we'll find any treasure?" I was imagining chests of gold and jewels. Dr. Hunter chuckled and pointed to the copy of *Treasure Island* lying on the table where I'd left it the night before.

"Been reading, have you?" I felt my face flush. "To be honest it's highly unlikely there will be anything a treasure hunter ... or even a pirate like Long John Silver ... would want aboard the *Intrepid*. But there will be plenty that is valuable — historically valuable that is. The artifacts will teach us about the community and culture of the crew. The ship's hull can tell an astute marine archaeologist how the ship was designed and built. Toolmarks will reveal woodworking techniques, and fragments of rigging, rope, or sails show how the ship was operated by the crew. In rare cases we find skeletons, and when we do they add to our understanding of how living and working at sea can impact the bones. At the same time I always keep in mind these bones are the remains of a real person, a sailor who lost his life to the sea and deserves proper respect." I thought of the ancient Coast Salish man Eddy and I excavated and knew exactly what Captain Hunter meant.

"Will you be taking artifacts back with you?"

"We'll assess it after we see what's down there, Peggy. Artifacts that have lasted this long in the salt water need special and immediate treatment once removed from the water. We might find metal, wood, bone, or leather objects that look in perfect condition, but without proper treatment after being brought to the surface, they can disintegrate before your eyes. We don't have the time or the equipment on this research trip to preserve anything too large, but we may find some small items that we can take back with us as evidence to support our find and use to gain financial backing from interested members of the public. You know, Peggy, this could become one of the most important shipwreck finds we've had in recent history."

Just then I was reminded about reading a book about a ship called the *Vasa*. It took decades for experts to conserve it. They had to keep the wooden hull under a constant spray of water and gradually introduced special preserving chemicals. Now the ship was one of Sweden's prime tourist attractions. My skin tingled thinking of how I was with the team of scientists about to discover an important shipwreck that could one day be British Columbia's most important tourist attraction. Maybe I'd get my picture in the paper ... or even better ... on TV.

It was getting late and Amanda said it was my turn to do prep for supper. I was supposed to get the potatoes peeled, carrots chopped, and lettuce washed. On my way to the galley I made a pit stop at the head. As I sat there relieving myself I got to thinking about what Captain Whittaker would think about us searching for his watery grave. I also thought about how much he and Aunt Beatrix had in common — like their whole "doing the right thing" moral code. I'd bet Aunt Beatrix would say Captain Whittaker was a man of integrity. I guess I would too.

When I finished I stood up and zipped my pants, then turned and flushed the toilet. "Wait! You idiot," I said as it dawned on me that I'd just flushed a huge wad of toilet paper. Amanda's cautious reminders clanged around in my head. Then I panicked. Surely the darned thing wasn't really as sensitive as she'd made it out to be. I pushed the flusher once more just to be sure it all went down. That's when I think my eyes momentarily popped out of their sockets as I realized the drain hadn't opened and the water level in the toilet bowl was quickly rising. I panicked and pushed the flusher again, but the drain still didn't open and now more water gushed into the toilet. Oh crap, that's when I remembered Amanda said to only flush once. That's also when I remembered my joke about this becoming the poop deck. Bewildered and a little scared I stepped out of the head and left just as water started to trickle over the top of the toilet bowl.

As I made my way to the galley, Aunt Beatrix nattered on and on in my head: "Be honest and face up to your mistakes" … "Face up to your problems with courage and remain honest and true" … "It's your moment-by-moment conduct that will determine the success of your life." Who said she got to be my conscience, I argued back. It's not my fault — someone should have fixed it. And besides, it might all settle and drain by itself. Why risk disappointing Amanda and Captain Hunter? Or for that matter, give Dr. Sanchez ammunition to prove he was right about letting a kid come on an important research trip.

I rummaged around until I found the potato peeler and peeled as fast as my fingers could possibly go. Then I washed and cut the lettuce and other vegetables, and set the pot of potatoes on the stove for cooking. I made my way to the stern where I would be alone. When — or if — the problem was discovered, I would simply say I'd been there for a long while reading and had no idea about the overflowing head.

It was a pretty big boat, but not big enough. Soon I heard yelling coming from down the hall and what sounded like cursing in Spanish. Then the boat slowed and stopped. I waited for what seemed like a reasonable time and then made my way towards the commotion, doing my best to look surprised.

"What happened?" I asked as Amanda and Scott mopped up water, and Captain Hunter banged inside the head with a wrench and hammer. I admit I had a twinge of guilt and almost confessed ... but when I saw the murderous look on Dr. Sanchez's face I couldn't.

"Best to just stay clear of the area, Peggy," said Amanda. "The head has flooded over. Do you know anything about it?" I shook my head vigorously ... maybe too vigorously.

Supper was very late that evening. By the time the mess was cleaned up and the food cooked everyone was exhausted and we ate in silence. Not Captain Hunter though, he was on deck taking the ship towards a little cove where we would let down our anchor for the night. I felt awful … but there was no point in telling the truth now that it was all over. It wouldn't make the situation any better and most definitely would make it worse — for me.

"Just to make sure we're all clear about this … the head is completely broken and off limits," the captain explained that evening. "From now on we will have to relieve ourselves in the bucket I've set out. I know it's a bummer, but not the end of the world, you know." He smiled at his little pun, trying to make light of the situation. Dr. Sanchez grumbled some more under his breath in Spanish. I did my best to block out an image of him reading the morning's newspaper while squatting over the mop pail.

As the light began to fade I felt the boat come to a stop and then the engine was shut off. "Okay crew, you know the routine," Captain Hunter announced. "After that let's get ready to tuck in. Tomorrow we visit Trust Island."

"We will?" I asked, suddenly feeling perked up.

"Correct, that's it over there — Tlatskwala," he told me, as he pointed towards the shoreline. "And somewhere nearby is a sunken ship … and I'm hoping very much it's the *Intrepid*." *Wow!* Instant goose bumps rippled up my arms and down my back. "In the morning we'll go ashore and meet with Chief Charles."

"Is that so we can ask for permission to dive in his ancestral waters?" I asked.

"That's exactly it. Some people might feel that these are national waters and they can do what they want. But I prefer to get the band's blessing. Besides that, I'm hoping they will be able to tell us something."

"You mean like stories from past generations of Kwakwaka'wakw who once lived here?"

"You got it, Peggy. I'm impressed that you are so aware of aboriginal concerns and rights." Captain Hunter patted my shoulder. I wondered if he'd say that if he knew it was me who broke the head. "Okay, crew, let's get going — we've got a big day tomorrow."

After I was in bed I pulled out Captain Whittaker's journal. I still hadn't found out what it was that sank the *Intrepid* and wanted to get to that part before seeing it at the bottom of the ocean.

"Don't stay up too long, Peggy. Tomorrow is going to be a big day," cautioned Amanda.

"Okay, I'll just read for a little while," I said, even though my eyes were already heavy and I was definitely ready for sleep.

March 17th, 1812

Things continue to be very tense aboard the Intrepid *and there is an air of uncertainty about the outcome of this voyage. Never have I had such a feeling of impending doom, and that our bad luck comes in the form of a certain gentleman.*

Now that we have entered northern waters the men are suffering from the extreme cold. March has always been a blowing month, but since we set sail from Big Island we have experienced a succession of hard gales and violent and icy rains. The ropes are near frozen each morning, the sails in desperate need of repair, and the sleet blinds our eyes. I feel ...

... My God, my hands are still trembling. I have just returned the ship to order after what was sure to be the scene of a murder. Mister Carver banged on my door an hour past to tell me the men were threatening to toss Mister Lockhart overboard. When I arrived on the scene they had him cornered and were demanding he give them leave of the blankets stored in the hold below. The foolish man was not the least afraid for his life, thinking somehow that the men were insincere in their threat. But I knew the look in their eyes to be desperate and feared mutiny had I not taken control that instant. I ordered Mister Carver to give each man one extra blanket and a coat. Mister Lockhart called me a cowardly dog as I tried to reason that his precious cargo was not worth his life, nor for that matter the life of my men. He argued that the crew had grown soft and I the cause. Then he swore he would have me decommissioned upon our return to New York. His threats were no match for the fear I felt for his life. He has no idea how close he came to dying this evening.

If we can but get ourselves ashore until the warmer winds prevail, my dear Mister Lockhart might just live

*to see us return to New York where he can do as he said
... report to Mister Astor that I have cost the company
a pretty penny in profit to save my ship and the lives of
my men.*

*For now order is restored and the men are quiet. I
have Mister Carver on guard outside Mister Lockhart's
quarters in case someone decides to retaliate further.*

Captain James Whittaker

I poked my head out and looked down at Amanda.
She was happily snoring. I knew that I should have
gone to sleep, but things were getting exciting and
I wanted to read just a little more of the captain's
log. As the pages turned it was like watching a TV
soap opera. Mister Lockhart was the nasty, trouble
making diva and Captain Whittaker was like the nice
one who had scruples, was conscientious, and loyal.
If I were to cast someone to be Mister Lockhart in a
movie I'd pick Dr. Sanchez. And starring as Captain
Whittaker — Dr. Hunter of course.

March 25th, 1812

*A week ago we found ourselves a safe place to anchor
and I sent six of my men ashore to get a lay of the land
and search for fresh water. Soon after their arrival they
were met by some local people. They call themselves the
Muhkaw and are a most genial tribe. They are middling
in stature, and of a dark complexion. I went ashore
and met with their chief, Snoqualmie. He was eager to*

introduce me to two clever young warriors. The youngest is called Loki and is about seventeen. He is the chief's son. He is stout, well-made, and fierce. The other lad is perhaps twenty, slight of stature, and smiles incessantly. His name is too difficult to pronounce and so the men have taken to calling him Peter. Of the two he speaks the best English. Both boys speak Chinook Wawa — a dialect commonly understood among many coastal tribes. As I observed them, they appeared unaffected by the cold despite their simple attire. In fact they appear to have no natural aversion or annoyances to the season at all.

Once I saw that they were sturdy and would be quite useful to us as interpreters I set about convincing Mister Lockhart. He pressed the chief to increase the count on furs and we nearly lost the deal. As it stands — in addition to the Muhkaw interpreters we are to receive one hundred otter pelts. In exchange Chief Snoqualmie is to get fifty knives, twenty flint, a sachet of buttons, a box of tinware, and twenty of our best wool blankets.

I made him a solemn promise that at the end of this expedition I would ensure his young warriors would arrive home safely. He held my hand firmly and gazed long and hard into my eyes. I understood immediately his intent and repeated my vow to bring the young men home. My word is all I have and I am grateful that it was all he needed to feel reassured.

We will stay here with the Muhkaw until the warmer winds blow. This will give us time to acclimate and fatten the livestock.

Captain James Whittaker

* * *

I could tell by the way Amanda was snoring that she was now in really deep REM sleep mode — probably where I should have been too. Okay, I promised myself — just one more entry from the captain's log and I'd turn off the light.

April 12th, 1812

Three days ago we had a near mishap after we stopped in a small bay. Loki and Peter went ashore with the crew. They are sturdy young men, but I can tell they miss the feel of solid ground. Then Loki went missing. When it was time to return to the ship he was nowhere to be found. Some of the men suspected he had deserted us — a suggestion made by Mister Lockhart. After a lengthy and thorough search for the lad Lockhart insisted he had indeed run away and that valuable time was being lost. He expected me to set sail without Loki. I daresay the gentleman still does not know me well. I could do no such thing after making a promise to his father. Until I was fully satisfied that nothing more could be done the ship would sail not a fathom. Then just before Mister Lockhart could protest further, out of the forest the lad emerged. Not only was he well, but draped over his shoulder was no less than a dozen otter pelts.

The next morning Loki and Peter communicated a deal with the Salish speakers and we are now 300 pelts richer. While Mister Lockhart was most pleased, he did not admit that it would have been a mistake had we actually left Loki behind. I daresay he completely forgot that he had suggested such a thing in the first place.

These warm winds are a welcome change to the ice and sleet and have created improved spirits amongst the men. Even Mister Lockhart himself has thawed somewhat.

Captain James Whittaker

CHAPTER SEVEN

While I was aboard the *Sea Weed* I felt fine, but the moment I stepped onto the dock my legs turned to rubber. As we walked up the gangway to meet Chief Charles I was worried they might collapse under me.

"Hello, Dr. Hunter and friends. Welcome," greeted the chief. As Captain Hunter introduced the team I took a moment to glance around. The village had a dozen small buildings, a longhouse, and some totems — many lying on their sides. For a moment it felt like we'd stepped back in time. I glanced out to where the *Sea Weed* was docked and wondered how far we were to the sunken *Intrepid*. I got goose bumps imagining it was two hundred years earlier and I was a Kwakwaka'wakw seeing the *Intrepid* the day it sailed into the inlet.

"Yes, we'd very much enjoy having a look around," Captain Hunter answered in response to the chief's invitation. We followed Chief Charles along a narrow pathway that led to the east side of the island. We stopped in front of what looked like an excavation site.

"You can see by these visible rows of rectangular house depressions that this was once a large and thriving community. Years ago some other archae-ologists came to excavate them and found a variety of things in different locations." We walked a little farther until we came to some grassy mounds with portions of exposed soil. "And here you can see one of the many shell middens — the rich black soil is full of cultural material, like whale bones. This was the place where my ancestors processed their food. The archaeologists studied the toolmarks on the whale bones to learn exactly how they were butchered." I bent over and fingered a number of dried bone fragments littered throughout the midden. I'd learned about shell middens during the excavation at Crescent Beach, which contained such things as crushed horse and littleneck clam, tiny fish vertebra, deer bone, and sometimes even human remains. No one knows for sure why the Coast Salish buried their dead in the middens — maybe to keep them away from wild animals. As I was thinking, my eye caught sight of a small blue object. I leaned in closer to check it out and suddenly my heart leapt.

"Captain, look!" I pointed until both the chief and the captain glanced down at the little gem at the end of my finger.

"Good eye, young lady ... you've spotted a trade bead. Over the years we've found hundreds — if not thousands — around our village. I'll show you later." Chief Charles then led us to a little white house that overlooked the ocean — a view Mom would say was worth millions. As we all crowded into the tiny kitchen, I noticed a little white-haired lady standing at the stove, frying something on an old black skillet.

Whatever she was cooking, it filled the room with a smell that was both sweet and oily.

"This is my mother, Passulip. She doesn't speak English too much. But she made you all some bannock — please sit and try her food." Once we were seated I took a piece of the warm flat bun and waited to see what the chief was going to do with it. "Come," he urged. "I'm sure you'll like it if you dip it in some cinnamon and sugar." I followed his lead.

"Mmmm, this is delicious," I mumbled between bites. "Almost like a donut." When Passulip smiled at me her eyes crinkled with laugh lines and her full brown cheeks caused me to smile too.

"Bannock is our traditional food — just not the cinnamon and sugar," said the chief. "But the young ones — they like it like this." While we ate, the woman poured dark tea into cups and added canned milk and honey. By the time we'd finished I was feeling warm and full.

As the adults talked I glanced around the kitchen. There was a stone bowl on the windowsill much like the kinds I'd seen at the museum. And wooden carvings and bone objects sat unceremoniously on top of the fridge, while on the wall hung a carved whale bone. Then something completely different caught my eye.

"What's that?" I asked, pointing to a round brass object that looked a bit like a compass. Passulip followed my eye to the object and then spoke to her son in her native language.

"Mother and I agree that you have a sharp eye. That came from the ship that you seek. It was given to our people by one of the European sailors two hundred years ago."

"May I look closer?" asked Captain Hunter. The chief passed the metal thing to the captain. "Fascinating ... this is a very old sextant ... the kind of navigational device commonly used by sailors during the seventeenth and eighteenth centuries."

"It was given in thanks to the chief who spared the lives of the survivors."

"Obviously with no ship they had no use for it — so it did make a very good thank-you gift. Does your mother have stories passed down to share about the sailors that visited here so long ago?" asked Captain Hunter.

The chief translated his mother's words in a slow and soothing voice. "The day the white men arrived was a day to remember," he said. "As the story goes their great canoe arrived in our cove under three small white clouds."

"Small white clouds? Do you mean sails?" I asked eagerly. Chief Charles smiled and nodded.

"Yes, young lady. But I prefer using the imagery of the old ones."

"Oh, right." My cheeks burned bright and after that I held my tongue as the chief continued telling his story.

"The elders said these men were a sight to behold — they were dirty, much too hairy, and smelled like rotting fish." A ripple of laughter spread throughout

123

the kitchen. "Among them was two of our kind and they talked in a language the people could understand. They said the white men wanted the furs of the otter. Our people were cautious, but they were also eager to make a trade for they were fully aware of the great treasures these men possessed. The traders made a bargain and did not keep it. This was a great insult to our chief and people. Some of the warriors snuck up on the ship that night to take what they were promised, but a battle broke out and many were wounded. Several of the warriors died and this caused the spirit of the sea to become angry and a great wind began to blow — it was so strong our people could hardly paddle back to the land. In the morning the ship was gone and the people thought the winds had taken it away. But soon things like wooden boxes, rope, and bales of otter fur started to wash up on our shores. Then my people found the camp of the white men and learned that their ship had sunk after striking the hidden rocks out by the point — the ones that stretch towards the sky like fingers from the sea. Over time many have tried to find the sunken ship but failed. Then about twenty years ago, some white people came to search too, but it was never found — that is until the day I called the salvage diver to come and untangle my fishing net and he found the anchor."

"Oh, you were the fisherman!" I said, surprised. "Do you know what happened to the crewmen who survived the sinking of the *Intrepid*?"

"Yes, Chief Noomki left the white men to camp not far from the village. The two Indian boys aboard the ship spoke on their behalf and the people took pity on them. The one called Loki stayed in our village long after the white men sailed away with a different ship. He married the chief's daughter — my great great grandmother." Chief Charles opened a small cabinet and removed a glass mason jar and gave it to Captain Hunter to look at. "Do you remember — I told you many small things have washed ashore or been found, like these glass beads."

"Aha," said Captain Hunter excitedly. I noticed the others sat up too. "These are definitely trade beads from China. They appear to be a type known as Fort Vancouver and were probably for necklaces. They're a single colour and would have been cut from a glass tube with six sides ... when it was new the facets would have sparkled." He opened the jar and poured some out. "You can tell they're hand polished because there are slight variations in size and shape." I picked up a few and rolled the little pearl-like beads around in my hand.

"During the fur trade they would have been strung together and sold by the fathom."

"A fathom?" I asked.

"Yes, a string nearly two metres long." After the captain closed up the jar the chief passed him a shoe box. When he lifted off the lid, lying in a bed of cotton were several pieces of broken china. I noticed how each was decorated with blue lines and figures.

"That's a cobalt blue glaze, right? It was supposedly first used a thousand years ago," I announced.

Wow! That's cool ... I actually remembered some of the boring stuff Aunt Beatrix told me. The captain seemed impressed.

"Good observation, Peggy. Maybe I should pair you with Scott, our pottery and ceramics expert." I wasn't sure if I was so keen about the idea of being stuck looking at broken teacups ... it sure wasn't any fun back at home. Nope, bones were my thing.

"Thank you for your hospitality today, Chief Charles. Now if I may, I ask for your permission to explore the traditional waters of the Kwakwaka'wakw to find the sunken *Intrepid*."

"You have our permission to search our traditional waters, Dr. Hunter," Chief Charles replied.

When we left the chief's house I paused for a moment. It was a magical moment there on the shore, looking out towards the sea. I thought of the people who once stood in the same place looking out to the same ocean, and how the waves that washed up on the shore now had done so two hundred years ago and two thousand years before that.

"Captain, when you find it how will you know that the ship is the *Intrepid*?" I asked as we boarded the *Sea Weed*.

"That's a good question. We know the *Intrepid* had three sails — something the chief's story just confirmed." *That's right,* I recalled — *three small white clouds.* "Some other things we'll be looking for are a box-like hull and six cannons. Most early trading ships had at least ten guns."

Captain Hunter steered the *Sea Weed* away from the shore and towards the coordinates he was given to find the anchor. With a good feeling about what we would find I sat on the deck with Captain Whittaker's journal. Now that we were at Tlatskwala Island I wanted to catch up to the part in the journal when the *Intrepid* arrived too.

May 13th, 1812

At last success is upon the Intrepid *and her crew. We have traded along the coast of New Caledonia and thus far acquired over eight hundred pelts of the finest grade. My crew — once agitated and dangerously close to mutiny — are content and put in fourteen to sixteen hours' work a day.*

It is a relief to see even Mister Lockhart is now usefully occupied in trading with the local people. There were some near disasters, but it appears he is acquiring the skills of a trader. While he is still aggressive in his approach there are fewer dangerous indiscretions, and he rarely disturbs the congenial interactions of the crew or the friendly nature of the aboriginals.

Intrepid's box-like hull and narrow stern enable us to maximize our profits by carrying the largest cargo with the smallest crew necessary. But our ship's hold is nearly full now and should we acquire many more pelts we may have to start storing them on the deck. We are equipped with three masts, which increases the ship's agility and speed significantly and will thereby shorten our journey across the

Pacific Ocean to the Orient. The one serious short-coming this grand ship has is that we are but lightly armed with only six guns — meaning we are not ideally suited for conflict in the unlikely event that one should arise.

I informed Mister Lockhart that we are near our maximum load and should soon make ready to sail for China. He is eager to make one more trade. The improved conditions aboard this ship have so affected us all that I agreed to his plan — mainly because we must make one final stop at the top of Vancouver's Island to wood and water for the long voyage ahead.

Our last trade was with the Tsaxis people — a very pleasant tribe. Loki and Peter were able to learn from them that there is a village a day's journey north. They believe it will make a most profitable final stop. We are now on route.

Captain James Whittaker

"I can't go with you?" I was crushed but did my best not to whine like Dr. Sanchez expected I would. I looked over at Amanda for support, but she only shrugged. "I thought that visibility is good — perfect diving conditions."

"That's right, it is. It's just that we don't know what's down there. Dr. Sanchez thinks we need to ensure the area is safe before taking a child — I mean a young person — down, and I agree." It figures that Dr. Sanchez was the one who wanted me out of the way. He'd been especially mean ever since the toilet got busted. I think he suspected I had something to do with it.

"Don't worry, Peggy, you'll get plenty of opportunity to dive once we know what's down there," Amanda said sweetly just before hopping over the side of the boat.

Disappointment washed over me as I watched the last of the crew disappear beneath the waves. A short while later, still in a foul mood, I heard the radio start to crackle and a disjointed voice calling through the static. I snapped up the handset and pressed the talk button.

"Hello?" I shouted to be heard clearly. The voice on the other side was faint and fuzzy so I turned some dials to make it come in clearer.

"Hello, is this Cap ... ter?" crackled a man's voice.

"No," I shouted back. "This is Peggy Henderson. Captain Hunter is diving right now."

"Fantast ...! Did ... find it?"

"Find it? If you mean the *Intrepid* — with my luck they probably found the ship and a ton of treasure too." I was still irritated over being left behind and I knew it was coming out in my voice but didn't care.

"Treasure! Right ...!" replied the crackling voice again. "That will make ... sound bite for ... evening's broadcast. So, Peggy ... you one ... researchers or ... treasure hunter?"

"Well, ah ..." I stammered, taken aback by the question. "Who is this calling, please?"

"Brad Turner, CFTV News — just try ... get the

scoop on the sunken ... everyone is talk ... 'bout. Tell me what the value ..."

"Hey, wait a minute," I shouted into the receiver when I finally clued in with horror who I was talking to. "You can't tell anyone what I just said. I'll get into trouble. I promised Dr. Hunter I could keep a secret."

"A secret, eh? Dr. Hunter must have something ... big going on at the bottom of the ... if you have to keep it such a ... You know, the public has a right to know Ms. Hender ... What would you say the value is of the treasure on ... *Intrepid*?"

"Wait, I didn't say there was treasure ... I just meant ..."

"Ms. Hender ... said they probably found treasure."

"No, I didn't mean that — I was just being sarcastic."

"Sounds more like you're trying to cover ... truth ... just come clean." I flicked the switch to silence the voice and the static, then slammed the radio handset down hard. *Good job, Peggy. News about the Intrepid could put the excavation at risk, but if people thought there was treasure — it could be a real disaster. I wouldn't be surprised if Captain Hunter thought it was me who tipped off the media in the first place.* Man, I was really going to have to walk the plank or become shark bait now.

As I considered my options I crossed off lying about it. I was already knee deep in guilt for busting the toilet and didn't think my conscience could handle another cover up. Nope, I definitely had to tell the captain … "come clean," as Brad Turner had said. But if I could only postpone the news until we got back to town …

I picked up Captain Whittaker's journal. I needed something to get my mind off the inevitable trouble I was in.

June 2nd, 1812

We have arrived at the place known as Tlatskwala Island. It is about eight leagues in length and four in breadth. While the ship sat a thousand feet from shore I noted some fifty or sixty armed people awaited us. At first we could not tell if they were there to oppose our arrival or to greet us. As we waited for some sign several of their men entered canoes and came out to the ship. Soon we were surrounded by them. I ordered my crew to toss over some trinkets to encourage good will. Even Mister Lockhart did not argue the matter with me.

Peter spoke to them and they seemed to understand that our purpose was to approach their chief with the prospects of a trade. It was a very friendly interview with the inhabitants and we were consequently invited ashore with a sampling of our trade goods.

The chief, who awaited our arrival, was brandishing a spear and wearing a cloth about his loins fabricated by grass. His nature seemed filled with prowess, irreverence even, and I thought to myself, there stands a magnificent man! Chief Noomki calls his tribe the

Kwakwaka'wakw and they appear to be a vibrant community. Despite all this, I do not feel an immediate report with them and sense they have no immediate feeling of kindness for us either.

We followed the chief to a large structure and entered. The image carved above the entrance was monstrous and quite intimidating to be sure. I was astonished at the size of the interior — the height about twenty-five feet. There were eight or ten enormous trees carved and painted into the forms of animals and humans, and served as house beams. They in turn were supported by planks of uncommon breadth and length. It is my estimate that some five hundred souls occupy the building. At the end of the long room Chief Noomki sat on a small platform, surrounded by many who appeared to be of significant rank.

We were invited to take part in a meal that consisted of boiled whale meat and fish soup eaten with mussel-shell spoons. After our meal the young men took part in a dance that involved drums, chanting, and remarkable masks — each with unique characteristics and vividly painted.

Tomorrow we will bring ashore more trade items. Loki tells me the chief expressed confidence we will be pleased with his otter pelts but he is looking for something significant in return. I cannot imagine what he hopes to get from us, but I should like to conclude our business with these people as quickly as possible. Mister Lockhart will negotiate the trade while I oversee the preparations for our voyage in two days time.

If matters go as planned the pelts will fetch a price

of twenty-five or thirty dollars apiece from the Chinese. That would bring nearly thirty thousand dollars in profit. Our aim is to bring back the most exotic textiles, ivory, brass, and chinaware — of which the ladies are so fond. Indeed, the set given me by the Emperor on my last voyage will make a handsome gift for my wife, Clara. Over the winter I intend to commission the same artisan to make additional pieces for the set.

Though I wish it were sooner, we shall not arrive at Canton until November. Tea shipments will be ready by then, however we will still have to winter there. In the spring we will use the northeasterly monsoon winds of the South China Sea to take us to Sunda Straight and then we shall ride the trade winds to the Indian Ocean and onwards to New York. After that I intend to give up this life at sea and spend my final years with my wife — perhaps I shall finally come to know my sons, Robert and James Junior. I dare say Mister Lockhart will be pleased with my retirement.

Captain James Whittaker

I sat dream-like under the warm sun while the gentle waves rocked me like a baby. For some reason I was thinking about my aunt's china when I heard the faint sound of splashing water. I hopped over to the side of the boat half expecting to see another pod of porpoises, but instead it was the team back from their dive. I should have been excited, but I only felt dread.

"Yahoo! It's amazing down there," Amanda gushed. "You're going to love it, Peggy." All the others were equally bubbling with enthusiasm over what they'd seen.

"Was it hard to find the anchor? Did you see the *Intrepid*?" I fired back.

"The anchor was right where our GPS indicated it would be — a perfectly spectacular example of one used on a seventeenth-century trading ship," Captain Hunter spouted while bobbing on the waves.

"And what about the *Intrepid*?"

"Not yet. We needed to set up the anchor as our datum point and start a radial grid with three metre intervals," said the captain. "Then Scott's tank ran low on oxygen so we had to surface. But we'll go down again this afternoon." I felt relieved they hadn't yet found the *Intrepid*.

"We saw a half a dozen artifacts already," Amanda said after she'd climbed up onto the boat.

"That's right. And now we've got lots to do to prepare for this afternoon. So Amanda and Marnie — you get started on the site map right away. Scott — I'll get you to prepare the lab and water treatment tank. And Dr. Sanchez — I'll need you to get on the radio and get the latest weather forecast from the Coast Guard. As we all know — weather around here can change quickly. I'll prepare the equipment for this afternoon's dive. Okay people, let's get to it."

"Ah, Captain, don't you have a job for me?" I asked, the disappointment swelling up again.

"Get the kid to make the food," said Dr. Sanchez. "It a safe place where she does no damage."

"Damage?" I said sharply. "Obviously you haven't

seen me cook yet." I stormed off towards the galley cursing the wiry little creep under my breath. A few moments later I felt a hand on my shoulder and turned to see Amanda. She was obviously amused.

"I bet you've some ideas of what you'd like to feed Dr. Sanchez."

"Yah — for starters, fish guts and boiled saltwater soup, followed by stuffed viperfish covered in ocean mucus and seasoned sand flies."

"Mmmm, sounds delicious. And for dessert?"

"Dessert will be fish eyeballs in Jell-O topped with whipped bilge water and shavings of ex-lax ... wait, better leave off the ex-lax ... the head is still broken." Amanda plugged her nose and we both laughed.

"Never mind Sanchez the Scrooge. Marnie's going to get started on the site map and I'll help you with lunch — I'm starved." We worked side by side to prepare the crew a tossed salad, grilled cheese sandwiches, and for dessert — banana bread. I really did wish we had some of that ex-lax on Jell-O for Señor Poop Head!

"Would you like to dive with me this afternoon?" Amanda asked while I set the table. I turned to face her instantly.

"This afternoon — really?" She nodded. "Captain said it was okay?"

"Sure, now that he's seen the terrain he feels it's safe for you to go down. Just promise you'll stick close and if you spot something, leave it in place for mapping."

Over lunch the conversation was focused on

the excellent condition of the anchor, the shredded rope still attached, and some mysterious wooden box about forty feet from it. The captain pulled out some charts that showed details of the depth of the seabed and ocean currents in the area.

"Will you try to bring the anchor up?" I asked.

"Not right now, Peggy. We don't have the right equipment to handle something so big on this trip. We'll need to leave it until we can figure out how best to move it."

Then Dr. Sanchez groaned. "Maybe the little girl should clear dishes so adults can talk business."

Amanda laughed. "No need, this is an equal opportunity crew," she said. "Hey Scott, I think it's your turn to do dishes."

"You got it. Hey, Marnie, will you give me a hand?" Scott and Marnie got up from the table and started to clear the dishes.

Dr. Sanchez groaned again.

"Captain, why don't you go ahead and finish what you were telling Peggy." Amanda winked at me.

"Sure, what I was saying is that the iron anchor has been sitting on the ocean floor for over two hundred years. If we just lift it to the surface and expose it to oxygen it would create a chemical change causing the iron to heat up. This would create intense internal pressure — so much that the anchor would crack into little pieces. "

"Is that what happens to wood too — does it just disintegrate?"

"Wooden artifacts preserved in perfect conditions

may look as good as new until taken out of the water — if allowed to dry they can split and collapse too. Generally, anything we recover from the sea must be given special preservation treatment from the moment it reaches the surface. Marnie, since you're our resident wood specialist, do you have anything else to add?"

"Well, Peggy, you can imagine that preserving an entire ship made of timber is a real challenge. It too would collapse into dust if it's not kept moist — so constant spraying is a first measure. Preserved timber can tell some pretty important and interesting things. For instance, by reading the rings on the timber — much the same way as tree ring dating — we can get a general date of when it was harvested — which in turn will tell us how old the ship is and possibly even where it was built."

"Scott, do you want to share something about glass and ceramics?" Amanda asked.

"I'd be happy to," Scott said, turning from the sink and wiping his hands on a dish cloth. "Glass and ceramics need to be stabilized and cleaned too. But the real danger is not usually oxygen, as in the case of iron and wood. The bigger problem here is that the glass and ceramics will have become brittle and fragile. Special care needs to be taken during excavation and during the cleaning stage too."

"If Marnie's specialty is wood, and Scott's is pottery and ceramics, then what's your specialty, Amanda?" I asked.

"My specialty? Human remains of course. And

from what Eddy told me, you're somewhat of an expert yourself." I smiled, but that quickly turned into a blush when I caught Dr. Sanchez sneering again.

"I wish someone had told me this was going to be a kids' day camp." I was happy when everyone ignored his comment.

"From what you've said, metals, wood, and ceramic could all be preserved in water given the perfect circumstances, but what about human remains?"

"Good question, Peggy. And the answer is — it all depends. Do you know what sailors used in the old days to preserve their food — meat in particular?"

"I think I read somewhere they used to use salt to keep meat from rotting."

"Right, it was the most efficient preservative they had aboard ships back then. The downside was the high salt content of the meat often caused sailors to have scurvy and high blood pressure. But getting back to preserving of human remains — salt water combined with an environment void of oxygen and some nice protective silt create the perfect place to preserve just about anything. Problem is — conditions are rarely so ideal. For instance, there are many organisms in the water that feed off organic matter. Dr. Sanchez can tell you more about that — his expertise is worms!" So that explained why the guy was so creepy.

"Worms! Nasty!" I said. Dr. Sanchez rolled his eyes. Captain Hunter grinned.

"It truly is fascinating stuff — go ahead, Hernado — we'd all like to hear about those nasty little creatures you find so interesting." More eye rolling and sighing.

"Yes, all right. My specialty is marine borers — poopilarly known as the sheep worm," he said in his heavy accent.

"*Poopilar sheep* worm?" I laughed. Probably shouldn't have.

"Not bah bah! I said *sheep* worm," he barked impatiently.

"He means 'ship worm,'" Amanda interpreted. "From your samples do you think ship worm is going to be a problem for us?"

"It's too early to say. The sheep worm cannot survive in certain types of water — like in brackish water. But let me tell you — if teredo and gribble worms are here then the timber from our *Intrepid,* she will be full of destructive tunnels — then it's going to go kaput if we take her from the water. My hope is the currents quickly covered her in silt before any sheep worms got to her. If so, then maybe we're going to find human remains."

"Say the preservation conditions are perfect — what's the chance we'll find human remains buried with the *Intrepid*?" I asked. Captain Hunter looked at his watch, his signal that it was time to wrap it up.

"Well, that's a good question, Peggy. And there's really no way of knowing until we find our ship. So I say we get going and do just that. Everyone with me?"

"Yes sir," I said, jumping up from my seat. "Let's get going ASAP!" The captain smiled. "Glad to hear you're in, Peggy. But first — Dr. Sanchez, what's the latest on the weather?"

"It's good for now, Dr. Hunter. But I want to say a something about the radio ... somebody's been touching all the dials. Was that you, *leedle* girl?" Zoom — my face turned the colour of tomato soup.

"Oh, yah, that. Ah, I was touching the radio because someone was calling. It was fuzzy so I turned some dials to try and get the reception clearer."

"You do not touch the radio, it is my job," said Dr. Sanchez. Then he looked over at Captain Hunter. "Yes, and his job too." He probably wanted to rag on me some more, but the conversation quickly turned to what needed to be prepared for the afternoon dive. After everyone split off in different directions to do their jobs Captain Hunter asked me about the call.

"You didn't say if you were able to make contact with the caller, Peggy." It was one of those split moment decisions — do I tell or not? After getting razzed by Dr. Sanchez I wasn't up to disappointing Captain Hunter at that moment. Especially not when everyone was in such a good mood and I was going to get my first chance to dive. It's not like there was anything he could do about it right then anyways.

"You know, the reception on that radio sure is bad," I said slowly. "It was hard to hear who was calling."

"Oh, I know, it can be pretty awful sometimes. Well, if it's something important they'll try again." He turned and headed off to the equipment room. *Hmmm ... that was easy*, I thought. And he had even jumped to that conclusion all by himself — now that can't be my fault. So then why did I hear Aunt Beatrix's words hounding me like a ghost: *Face up to your problems with courage and remain honest and true. If nothing else, remember it's your moment-by-moment conduct that will determine the success of your life.* What a pain having Aunt Beatrix for a conscience!

CHAPTER EIGHT

Glancing up towards the ocean surface I saw a beautiful blanket of emerald green light. It was bright enough to illuminate all the little particles floating around me, but not enough to light the dark ocean floor below. For that we needed waterproof flashlights. As the rays from the flashlights lit the sandy surface I saw the anchor for the first time and was surprised at how small it was — I was expecting something at least as big as a Volkswagen. Then I noticed the circular grid the team started that morning. It looked like a giant spider web with the anchor caught in the middle. Not far was a reef loaded with marine life, including patches of violet coral, blue-clawed crabs, and plumose anemones.

Before our dive Amanda warned me to not interfere with any of the sea life — especially the anemones. She also made me review hand signals and the four points a diver must always keep in mind — depth, air, time, and area. I half expected she'd pull a Tornado and make me write DATA on my hand, but she didn't. But that's when I learned that the fun and carefree Amanda was all business when it came to diving.

"Don't feel bad, Peggy. I do this with all my dive partners. You don't want to be fifty feet under water and be confused over the safety details or what your partner's trying to communicate to you."

With everyone now all paired off, Captain Hunter gave us the signal to fan out from the anchor and do a visual search of the area. As each team swam away in different directions I hoped Amanda and I would be the ones to find the ship first — not that it was a race, but it would probably annoy Dr. Sanchez. We knew that the ship couldn't be too far but visibility was poor that afternoon and we couldn't see more than ten feet ahead ... which was why I practically hung on to Amanda's flippers. There was no way I wanted to get lost down there!

As we swam slowly along Amanda stopped frequently to jot notes on her waterproof permatrace paper. At first I didn't see anything too noteworthy, but then I realized that what appeared at first to be only small mounds covered in sea plants could very well be man-made objects — otherwise why would Amanda plot them on her grid? I had the urge to brush away the silt and sea weeds to see if they really were artifacts, but I knew better than to disturb the site. Eddy always told me that artifacts *in situ* could tell an archaeologist a lot. I was pretty sure that rule applied to underwater archaeology too.

Before swimming away from each artifact Amanda signaled for me to me push in the small markers with orange ribbon tied to them. Later, when the team came back to do a full-scale excavation those little markers would help her to locate the artifacts again.

When I shoved in that first marker I felt like Neil Armstrong planting the American flag on the moon.

We came to a place that looked like an underwater secret garden with five stone steeples, each decorated with a kelp fringe and coral growing in between. The huge stones looked like church spires reaching up towards the ocean's surface. As we stared up at them Amanda turned to me — but before she could give me a sign I knew what she was thinking. I took her perma-trace pad and pencil and wrote in block letters: THE HIDDEN ROCKS THAT SANK INTREPID. She nodded and I could see inside her mask that her eyes were wide with excitement. She gave me the thumbs-up sign and then jotted the coordinates on her water-proof pad. We were swimming around the outside of the rock pinnacles when I looked down at my watch and then my gauge — we only had ten minutes left before we would have to surface. Amanda noticed too.

We were about to turn around and swim back towards the anchor when I noticed an unusual shape a short way from the pinnacles. I signed to Amanda that I wanted to check it out. I thought she might say no, but then she noticed it too. We swam over to look closer at the cross-like feature that was as thick and long as a telephone pole. Like everything else we'd seen, it was covered in fine silt, and plants and tiny fish had claimed it as home. I could feel my heart rate quicken as we swam the length of it — here and there peeking from out of the silt were pieces of thick rope, pulleys, and metal parts. Then there it was ... a box-like hull resting silently on its side. It was both amazing and scary and while I was definitely excited to see it I also felt solemn — the way I did on Remembrance Day while standing at the cenotaph with Uncle Stewart.

Amanda gave me an underwater high-five. I don't know if her heart raced like mine, but I knew all this excitement was costing us oxygen. She tapped her watch — the signal that our time was up. I could tell that she didn't want to leave any more than I did, but neither of us was so foolish as to ignore the gauge on our oxygen tanks. We swam back towards the anchor where the others had reassembled. Then in pairs we made the ascent to the ocean surface. As soon as we reached the surface we both pulled our mouth pieces out and were shouting "Yahoo" and splashing around like little kids. When it became clear what we were so excited about everyone else started to cheer and high-five too.

That night we celebrated — pan-fried fish and chips with tartar sauce, plus Marnie whipped up one of those chocolate fudge cakes in a box for dessert. We sat around the galley table for hours and I listened as the crew told stories about other underwater excavations they'd been on. Even Dr. Sanchez had some interesting things to tell about a Spanish galleon he'd worked on in the Sea of Cortez. But what I enjoyed the most was listening to Captain Hunter tell about his work on the *Mary Rose* — the sixteenth-century British battleship that now sat in a museum that was built especially for it.

"You know, one of the most amazing things we found among the 19,000 artifacts collected from that wreck was a glass jar. When we opened it — five hundred years later — we could still smell the menthol inside," said the captain. "And as for the human remains — well, not only did the thick silt preserve the structure of the *Mary Rose* and all she contained, but the men trapped on board when she sank." I realize other kids might find it morbid to hear all the icky details of the six skeletons they found clustered around the cannon on the main deck of the *Mary Rose* — but not me. I wanted to know every bone deep fact!

"Human bones can tell a lot about a person's life," continued the captain. "The remains we found on the *Mary Rose*, for instance, showed us they were big, strong men used to heavy work — like loading and firing a two-tonne bronze gun. And being a soldier on a sixteenth-century battleship was no place for the old — which was why most of the remains found were of men under the age of thirty. One was a thirteen-year-old boy." *The same age as me,* I thought. "I love this work because it opens a window to the past and reveals a very human story about what life was like back then — the strain and injuries they endured, their poor diets. And the artifacts are revealing too — like in the master carpenter's chest we found a sundial, a book, and a backgammon set — a sign of wealth for that time."

"Do you think the Intrepid will have some good stories to tell us too?"

"Oh, I'm sure of it, Peggy."

I knew sooner or later I had to tell Captain Hunter about spilling the beans to the reporter, but I just couldn't seem to find the right moment. Then suddenly everyone was toddling off to bed to rest up for the big dive the next day. Now that we had located a ship, the next step was to confirm that it was in fact the *Intrepid*. And that was definitely something I didn't want to miss.

After everyone had turned in for the night I lay on my bunk with Captain Whittaker's journal. I had only a few pages left to read and I was anxious to get to the end.

June 24th, 1812

Mister Lockhart is a scoundrel and has catastrophically botched negotiations with Chief Noomki by promising weapons and ammunition. When I learned about the deal I went ashore to explain to the chief that the weaponry we have is destined for elsewhere. He mistook my intentions as an attempt to drive up the bargain. By all that I have seen these Kwakwaka'wakw people are well-off. I do not fully understand their desire to possess guns except to exert their power over rival tribes. A trade such as this would only create an imbalance amongst the coastal people and upset the natural order. I cannot in good conscience be part of such a bargain. Our interpreters, Peter and Loki, have done their best to convey my regret to the chief. To temper his mood I made him an excellent offer for copper pots, tinware, buttons, and blankets — a better deal than made to others — but I could see by his ingenuous demeanor that he was lost to us.

When I returned to the ship I found Mister Lockhart so intent on completing the trade that he was threatening the men with dire consequences unless they started unloading muskets and gunpowder. He soon discovered their loyalty to me runs deep.

Peter tells me that Chief Noomki perceives the broken deal as deeply humiliating and retaliation is likely. I too sensed that the chief is a dangerous man and I feel it prudent to make preparations to set sail at first light. I should like to navigate the ship to a safer distance from shore, but a storm is moving in and I am also worried about an outcropping of rocks that were observed when the tide was low. For now, the ship is well anchored and I have set Mister Thomas on first watch, and Mister Barry at the entrance of the ammunitions room. While I do not trust the chief, I trust Mister Lockhart even less.

Tomorrow, when all of this is behind us, I will decide what is to be done with him. I am now convinced that every man on this ship is doomed should we continue with him aboard. I will consider my options once we are safely on our way.

Captain James Whittaker

As I came to the end of the page I realized something. To be sure I was correct I counted on my fingers starting from the day we'd left the docks at Steveston. Then just to be double certain I counted a second time. There was no mistake — the date on the page I'd just read in the captain's log was June 24th— the same date as today. As this idea settled in my mind I couldn't decide if this coincidence was a good thing or not. Then it occurred that the next day was even more significant — because it was on June 25th that *Intrepid* sank. Now I'm not a superstitious type, but I decided not to read the final entry — at least not until after our dive the next day. I closed up the captain's log, shut off the light, and put my head down on my pillow. As the boat swayed gently to and fro I looked out the small window beside my bed, noting how eerily quiet it was and how there was nothing to see, for it was a perfectly black night — if such a thing could be perfect.

The next morning everyone was buzzing around in preparation for the big dive. Since I didn't have much to do I volunteered to cook up some scrambled eggs and toast while they got ready. Over breakfast the conversations were flying around the room. The captain gave everyone instructions for what they were to do during the dive. Amanda reminded Scott to bring the extra waterproof camera. And Dr. Sanchez gave the latest weather report.

"For now it's perfect weather, Dr. Hunter."

"Great. Well, team ... let's go!" Just as everyone set off to get into their wet suits the captain caught me by the arm. "Peggy, I got the feeling there was something you wanted to talk to me about last night." I hoped the captain didn't notice that my cheeks were suddenly flushed.

"Well, there is something I want to discuss. I just think it would be better if I waited until afterwards." I was glad that he accepted my response for it was definitely not the time for a confession.

The surface visibility that morning was poor, but as soon as we'd descended to the ocean floor we could see as far as a hundred feet or more. The wreck was perched on a shallow ledge, where the fast currents had transformed it into a living reef. The wooden hull lay blanketed with fine silt and the stern was covered with ghostly white plumose anemones. Schools of black rockfish hovered over it until they sensed our presence and instantly disappeared.

I was a little jealous that everyone on the team had a job except me. I watched as Marnie and Scott silently criss-crossed the wreck with measuring tapes in order to create a grid. Dr. Sanchez was taking samples of the wood and storing them in small vials. And while Captain Hunter took photographs Amanda made diagrams and notes.

I was free to explore the area as long as I didn't swim out of sight. I swam to the quarterdeck of the ship where I noticed a door. It must have settled in an open position when the ship landed on its side two hundred years earlier. I gingerly thrust my flashlight into the cavern to see what was inside. As my eyes settled on the dimly lit space I could see a cabinet and bookshelves, and then an overturned table, and a high-back chair. As I stared into that silent room it slowly dawned on me I was looking into the captain's quarters. Then a vision flashed through my mind of Captain Whittaker sitting at that wooden table writing in his captain's log ... right up to the hours before the ship sank. It was a sight that was sort of creepy, but at the same time squeezed on my heart.

When I felt a hand on my shoulder I jumped. It was only Dr. Sanchez giving me the "get lost" sign. I'd have given him a hand sign of my own, but just then a really gross looking fish darted out of the door and swam towards the stern. I followed after him, determined to get a good look so I could identify the species later. He took off over the quarter-deck and then swam towards the stern. As I pursued him he led me down the back of the ship and then slipped from my view.

I scanned the area to see where the slippery little devil had gone. As I searched on the back side of the ship I realized the others wouldn't be able to see where I was. I didn't want to cause concern so I made my way back towards the side of the ship where they were working. As I swam something vaguely familiar caught my eye. Really, I'd seen it so briefly that it nearly didn't register. But a small voice in my head told me to swim back for a closer look.

All mammal skeletons — whether they're seals, monkeys, or humans — share similarities. Take the vertebrae for example — all animals have back bones that are basically the same shape. Then there's the long bones — like the radius, ulna, and humerus

— that are generally similar too. But there's one thing that is unique to humans: it's our long and opposable thumbs. Those two little appendages allow us to thread a needle, paint beautiful images, write with a pen, and throw a curveball.

And it was just such a neat little row of thumb bones — the first and second phalange, the meta-carpal and carpal — that caught my eye in that split second while swimming by. When I turned around and came back for a slower, second look sure enough there it was — a thumb, protruding from the silt like a hitchhiker. I didn't know if it was a good idea or not, but I took off one of my flippers and used it to fan the silt and sand surrounding the bones. While I waited for the murky cloud to settle I had to keep reminding myself not to hold my breath. When the sand finally cleared from the water I could see the bones of an entire human hand. I excitedly fanned the silt again … and this time I could see that the tiny hand bones were attached to a radius and ulna. Then something shiny caught my eye — as I looked closer I could see it was a single brass button. The kind found on a uniform — like maybe the cuff of a captain's uniform. I double inhaled then exhaled slowly as the idea settled in my mind that there was a good chance that if the rest of the sand were removed it would reveal a complete human skeleton — and there was a good possibility it was Captain Whittaker's.

When I reached Amanda I tugged impatiently on her arm. She signaled to wait while she finished up her diagram of the main mast. But instead I pulled the pencil from her hand and made her follow me. I could tell she was annoyed as I led her to the back of the hull where the bones waited. I knew she wouldn't be mad for long — and I was right.

After letting out enough air bubbles to fill a bathtub she took out her measuring tape and notepad. While she made notes and a quick sketch I dragged Captain Hunter, Marnie, and Scott to see what I'd found. I even reluctantly encouraged Dr. Sanchez to come, but he gave me the "beat-it" signal again. It wasn't until Captain Hunter went for him that he got to see what everyone else was so excited about.

The worst part about doing underwater archaeology is that you can only stay under the water for a little while. And then you have to wait several hours before diving again — that's so your body can release the build-up of nitrogen gases that come from breathing compressed air. As we all slowly ascended to the surface I was pretty sure they all felt the same as me — wishing that we didn't have to go.

Feeling pretty proud for being the one with the sharp eye, I let everyone else climb aboard the *Sea Weed* first. I was sure they were all really glad now that I had come along — even Dr. Sanchez. So while I climbed up the ladder I half expected they'd all applaud me. But when I finally hauled myself onto the deck they were all listening carefully to the captain, who was on the radio talking to someone.

"Thanks for the heads up, Professor Blake. I will look into it." The captain's face was stern when he turned and looked over at me.

"Peggy, that was one of my colleagues at the university. He says there was a report about the *Intrepid* on last night's news. The reporter quoted one of the researchers — Ms. Peggy Henderson — saying that there was treasure found on the shipwreck. Why do you think he said that?"

It's funny how one minute everything is going spectacularly and everyone thinks you're a hero. Then something happens and you're worse than dog poop stuck to the bottom of their boots.

It wasn't surprising that the captain was mad. But what really hurt was that he believed I just wanted to be in the spotlight and was the one responsible for spilling the beans earlier in the week about the search for the *Intrepid*. When I tried to convince him differently, he dropped another bombshell.

"Peggy, maybe if you hadn't lied about plugging the head the other day I would be willing to believe you're as innocent as you say you are. But since I know as well as you do that you were responsible I'm having a hard time accepting what you're telling me." I suddenly felt like I was eight again and Mr. Munro had caught me with a bag full of Honey Nut Cheerio samples I'd stolen from from all the neighbours' mailboxes.

"If you knew it was me that busted the toilet why didn't you say?" I whispered.

"I was hoping that you were conscientious enough to tell me about it yourself — in fact that's what I thought you were going to do last night. But now I see there's a pattern of deceptiveness going on here and I just don't think I can trust you anymore. There's too much at stake here."

After lunch the captain informed me that for the rest of the day I was grounded — if that's possible on a boat. Amanda, Scott, Marnie, and the captain would go back down, while I stayed behind — a consequence I knew I deserved. I hadn't meant for things to go so horribly wrong. Now I would have to face Eddy and my mom and aunts, who'd be disappointed in me — again. Then like adding salt to an open wound, Captain Hunter told me that Dr. Sanchez would be staying to keep an eye on me. That's because I'd lost the captain's trust, and that hurt more than anything.

CHAPTER NINE

"Peggy, these artifacts are really fragile and unstable. So you'll need to rinse them as gently as possible to remove all the salt water. It's going to take several repetitions of rinsing and draining to make them saline free. When we get them back to the university lab I'll immerse them in some polyethylene glycol to reinforce the cellular structure." The artifacts Amanda left me to clean were a small leather pouch, a piece of braided rope and a tiny porcelain dish.

"I don't think it's a good idea," Dr. Sanchez rattled on. "She is just a kid and she is going to make some more damage." That was a crushing blow to my already bruised ego.

"Don't worry, I know that Peggy can do this," Amanda encouraged. I appreciated her confidence, but wasn't sure that I deserved it. I mean how many kids get an opportunity to go on a trip like this and then blow it so fantastically?

While I worked alone in that little room I pictured everyone else diving in the deep waters below and looking over the amazing skeleton I'd found. While I was distracted by my miserable mood I overfilled one of the trays. As I mopped up the water I knew I couldn't afford to screw up anything else, so I made myself focus on what I was doing.

Each artifact that Amanda wanted me to clean was in its own small tray filled with tepid clear water. With tongs I gently swished the leather pouch around then let it sit while I did the same with the other two artifacts. Next, I had to drain the water off and then fill the trays again with new clear water. I did that a lot of times. And as I did I could see that the small plant matter and grains of silt and salt were slowing becoming dislodged and the finer details of each object were coming into view.

I got really curious about the leather pouch. It had a small flap and under it a drawstring pulled tight. I could see there was some kind of design on the flap. I also felt something squishy inside. As I continued cleaning I soon realized it wasn't a design on the flap, but rather someone's initials in large italic letters — R.L. As soon as I realized what it was I went for Captain Whittaker's journal and flipped to the list of crewmembers at the back. I already knew one person who had those initials, but I had to check to see that there weren't others. As my finger ran down the list I had a warm feeling of excitement — the kind that came from discovering something new. While there was one crewman whose last name started with an L — assistant boatswain, Mister Daniel Lawrence — there was no one else. I let the facts slowly sink in. There was only one person on the ship who had those exact initials — Robert Lockhart — a.k.a. Mister Lockhart.

I took a small pair of tweezers and gently folded

back the flap and then carefully loosened the tie. Holding up the dripping bag I looked inside and saw a dark brown sludge that looked a lot like coffee grounds, but smelled just like my Uncle Jerry. He smoked two packs of cigarettes a day. Tobacco — that was what was inside! My mind flashed back to when Captain Whittaker wrote in his journal about the cook's boy stealing a pinch of tobacco from Mister Lockhart's pouch and that later he had to whip him for it. I shook with excitement as I gently retied the pouch and returned it to the water. This was certain to be the kind of evidence Captain Hunter needed to prove that we'd found the *Intrepid*.

I decided to turn my attention to the other artifacts to see what they could tell me. But just as I was changing the water again I heard the sound of a motorboat getting closer and closer. I peered out the lab window but couldn't see anything. Then I heard strange voices followed by angry shouting. I ran down the corridor and up the stairs to the deck. By the time I got there, Dr. Sanchez was yelling at the top of his lungs at a man on the other boat who was holding out a microphone. Not far to his right was another guy filming them with a video camera. The letters on the side of the camera read CFTV.

"Oh great," I groaned. I'm not sure if what I did next was a good idea, but I had to do something to try and help clean up this mess I'd created. "Ah, Mr. Turner," I called out. "I'm Peggy Henderson. I talked to you the other day." Brad Turner looked at me and grinned.

"You? You're Peggy Henderson?" Then the laughter disappeared and his voice took on an irritated edge. "Well, you're nothing but a kid. What kind of an operation is this? What about that treasure?" Dr. Sanchez started shouting again, this time in Spanish. That's when I walked over to him and put my hand over his mouth. I watched his eyes open to the size of golf balls and thought he might bite me. But it was a risk I needed to take.

"Please, Dr. Sanchez. Let me say something," I pleaded. I then turned back to the reporter. "Look, Mr. Turner. There is no treasure. There never was. There never will be. I just said that because I was … well …" I could feel my face was on fire, "… a silly kid, who didn't know she was talking to a news reporter. But mister, you were the one who took the things I said and twisted them up. And while I'm on the subject, aren't you supposed to identify yourself before starting to ask questions? I mean isn't there some code of ethics you're supposed to go by? If I'd known you were a reporter I wouldn't have said anything. And you know why? Because this is an important scientific research trip to find a shipwreck that could have great historical significance to the people of Canada … heck, what am I saying … to the people of North America. By letting the public know about what we're doing before we're ready, you've put the *Intrepid* and all that she holds at risk. People who don't know any better may come here and start helping themselves to parts of the ship or take artifacts for souvenirs — and if they do they're taking something that belongs to us all — our history. Do you want to be responsible for that, Mr. Turner?" The cameraman lowered the camera.

"Hey, Brad. Do you want me to keep filming this?" Brad dropped the microphone and shook his head.

"Nah, it looks like this was a big waste of time and money, Charlie. If there's no treasure — there's no story. Nobody cares about history. C'mon, let's get out of here. Maybe there's still time to find another story for the evening news. Otherwise the boss is going to have my head." While their boat turned around Dr. Sanchez couldn't resist the chance to tell them off one last time.

"You are a stupid TV guy. Just get out of this place and stop making problems."

"Ah, Dr. Sanchez, I don't think they can hear you ... maybe you should try yelling a little louder," I snickered. I think he was about to turn on me, but he caught himself and I watched the anger drain from his face.

"Funny, funny, *leedle* girl." Then he smiled at me for the first time since we'd met. Just as I was enjoying this new side to Dr. Sanchez the radio started to crackle. When we got to the helm we heard a barely audible woman's voice speaking in an urgent tone. Dr. Sanchez turned the dials to fine tune the signal, but we could still only make out parts of the message.

"... Guard. Storm ... Northern Vancouver Island ... small craft ... I repeat, this is the Coast ... Storm clouds moving in quickly ... all small crafts should find shelter immediately." Dr. Sanchez looked to the west where a wall of dark clouds moved towards us. I looked at my watch.

"When are the others supposed to resurface, Dr. Sanchez?"

"I think not for another half hour." There was nothing we could do except wait. It was both eerie and amazing how quickly those clouds approached and the wind-whipped waves picked up. Minute by minute I watched as the swells grew larger. In the back of my mind I was starting to wonder how everyone was going to get back up onto the boat. I got a chill when I remembered that it was the very same day two hundred years ago that the *Intrepid* went down.

"Dr. Sanchez, do you think maybe we should call the Coast Guard?" Outside the wind was beginning to howl and my heart rate was rising fast. "My sailing teacher told me it's better to call sooner than later. If we wait until we're in deep trouble it might be too late to get help."

"Okay, this is a good idea. I make the call and you batten down the hatches. We need to be ready to go as soon as the others surface." I went around the entire boat closing and latching cupboards, windows, and doors. Then I put the loose items away and made sure everything else that might go flying was secured. That was when I remembered the artifacts soaking in water — as I ran towards the lab I was hoping that they hadn't already been thrown to the floor. When I got there I found all three of the trays had slid down to one end of the counter. They were sure to have slipped off if I hadn't been there. I looked around for some way to secure them. There was only one thing I could think to do. I opened the plastic garbage pail and emptied the waste into the sink. Then I picked out the plastic bag inside and filled it with clean water. As gently as possible I transferred each of the three artifacts into the water-filled bag and tied it tight. Then I set it back in the garbage pail and rammed it in the corner to keep it from sailing around the room.

After that I waited with my eyes peeled for the team to come to the surface. Getting them on board was going to be tough. It wasn't long when I heard Dr. Sanchez shouting: "They're here! Quick, they're here!" I ran to the stern where the ladder hung over the side — but it wasn't going to do them much good. I watched Amanda and the others being tossed roughly on the waves. I'm sure it was as clear to them as it was to me that if they didn't time their entry just right they could be sucked in under the boat or thrown hard against it.

"It's going to be too dangerous for them to come up the rope ladder, Peggy. And they are getting tired."

"What about the Coast Guard?" I shouted back.

"They're not going to be here for a while yet. So we've got to do something." As Dr. Sanchez prepared to toss the boat's life rings out to them my adrenaline-fogged mind searched for a better solution. That's when I saw the tarp that was covering the old fishing net and remembered that the *Sea Weed* was really a fishing boat. I looked up to the trawler cables and wondered …

"Dr. Sanchez, do you know how to operate the trawler winches?" He looked at me like I'd lost my marbles. "Look, if we rig up that net to one of those trawler arms we could lower it into the water. They'll be able to grab onto it at a safe distance from the boat and then we can haul them up on deck."

"You're right, *leedle* Peggy girl. It's a good idea!" He slapped me on the back and almost sent me flying.

As the wind and waves whipped us around we dragged that old net over and hooked it to the cables. A few minutes later it was rising off the deck and being dropped over the side of the boat. I watched as everyone swam over to it and grabbed on. The trawling arm effortlessly lifted the team up out of the water and dropped them onto the deck like a load of fresh salmon. As I helped them get untangled Dr. Sanchez went to draw up the anchor. Soon after, the Coast Guard arrived and led us slowly to the safety of Tlatskwala inlet.

That night Chief Charles invited us to sleep in the Kwakwaka'wakw longhouse. When we entered I noticed the place smelled of fresh cedar and smoke. Later, as the wind and rain beat against the building we all huddled close to the fireplace where the flames flickered and crackled. The band members had kindly provided us with stew and biscuits for dinner. Later, while I sipped on some hot chocolate I studied the totem poles that sat at each end of the longhouse. I was hoping maybe later Chief Charles would come and tell us their stories.

"Peggy, you did some pretty quick thinking back there." Captain Hunter sat down on the floor beside me.

"I'm just glad I could help, Captain." For once I didn't mind that my face was as red as a beet.

"And Amanda told me what you did to protect the artifacts. That was ingenious."

"Are they okay? I hope they didn't get damaged."

"Actually, they're so well protected we decided to leave them that way until the storm lets up." We sat quietly side by side for several minutes, mesmerized by the bright firelight.

"I'm really sorry for lying to you, Captain," I said quietly. "I should have told you right away about the toilet and the news reporter. I guess I was afraid that I'd be a disappointment." The captain leaned over and ruffled my hair.

"Well, you might be surprised, but I have an apology to make too. You see, Dr. Sanchez finally revealed that he was the one responsible for the leak to the media. He was talking to some friends, thinking they would understand the importance of keeping his news secret, but obviously they didn't. So when Brad Turner called he deliberately tried to sound like he was connected to our project. You couldn't have known what he was up to."

And there you go — suddenly I was no longer dog poop stuck to someone's boot.

"I haven't read the last few pages of Captain Whittaker's journal. Do you think we could read them together now?" I asked.

"Great idea, young lady. Folks, gather round. We're going to have a bedtime story."

I took out Captain Whittaker's journal from my bag and turned to the last few pages. It was weird being there in the Kwakwaka'wakw longhouse — not far from the captain's watery grave, reading by fire-light his last tragic words — words written just a short while before the *Intrepid* sank and he was to die.

"June 25th, 1812," I began. *"In our hasty departure from Tlatskwala Island the Intrepid struck an outcrop of submerged rocks that tore open her hull. We are taking on water to the measure of two feet an hour and there is little time left for us.*

"In this, my final entry as captain, I accept full responsibility for our present calamity...."

When I finished reading the page no one said a word. It was almost like there was an understanding that the occasion deserved a solemn minute of silence in honour of Captain Whittaker and all those who died that night.

"We're so close to the end now, why don't you read the last couple of pages to us, Peggy?" asked Amanda.

"Okay," I said, and then I continued reading.

June 29th, 1812

As instructed by Captain Whittaker I will do my best to make good on his final orders and see that this journal reaches New York City and the owner of the American

Fur Company, Mister John Jacob Astor. The crew made it safely to shore after Captain Whittaker ordered us to abandon ship. For now, the Kwakwaka'wakw have allowed us to camp here on their island unharmed. Credit for our safety goes to Loki and Peter, who pleaded on our behalf. Were it not for them I am certain I would not be writing this entry today. We are not sure how long their goodwill can last, but they have a great interest in Mister Hughes, our blacksmith. He is teaching some of them to forge fish hooks and other such metal objects. In addition, Chief Noomki's daughter has shown interest in Loki and I think he fancies the young lady, too. We shall see what comes of the romance, but it is a most delicate situation to be sure.

The dispute with the Kwakwaka'wakw arose a few days ago after Mister Lockhart promised to sell weapons and ammunition to the chief. Captain Whittaker vehemently rejected the arrangement when he learned of it. His refusal to allow the sale of arms to the Kwakwaka'wakw led to misunderstandings and stirred up wrath amongst the chief and his men who believed Captain Whittaker and Mister Lockhart were breaking the arrangement only to press for more otter pelts. As First Mate, I am certain this was never Captain Whittaker's intent, but the die was cast and there was no starting afresh.

It would be remiss to not comment on Captain Whittaker's honourable conduct in the hour prior to the Intrepid's *sinking. As he stated, we were boarded by the aboriginals unexpectedly while most of the crew were below deck asleep. The captain himself was awake in his quarters having felt uneasy over the anger expressed by Chief Noomki and the Kwakwaka'wakw. It was his plan that we leave at first sight of dawn and he was charting our course when the attack broke out.*

By the time the crew realized what was happening, it was too late for poor Mister Thomas, who captain had put on watch. What Mister Robert Lockhart was doing on deck at that time is a mystery to us all. With great effort we managed to regain control of the ship and sent a strong message by firing our cannons at them. The captain feared there might be a second attack at dawn and ordered the men to draw up the anchor and prepare to set sail. Unfortunately luck was not on our side and as soon as our anchor was on board a great wind picked up and we were faced with fierce swells that tossed us about. It was in such a storm that we began our departure from the sheltered bay of Tlatskwala Island. The captain set our course so as to go well around the rocks we knew were nigh below the water's surface. But the blinding storm and the black night proved to be a worse foe than the Kwakwaka'wakw.

At the moment we struck the rocks the force was so great that the main mast snapped in two, the men and cargo were tossed in the air and even the anchor was hurled over the side like it was a mere toy. The captain quickly assessed the damage and could see the ship was lost to us. He ordered the men to evacuate and soon the Intrepid's *lifeboats were precariously overfull. Even though the men begged him, the captain vehemently refused to abandon the* Intrepid, *stating it was his duty to go down with her. He then ordered we cast off without him and wished us well.*

As the ship slipped out of sight the captain stood on the quarterdeck and raised a cup to us all, as though he were toasting us. It was both a noble and peculiar sight. "Carry on lads," he shouted. "Live on and make me proud." Every man who was there saluted, and even the boldest shed a tear.

Losing the Intrepid *and her worldly goods was a tragedy to be sure, but a far worse thing is having lost Captain James Whittaker. He lived his life with honesty, diligence, and courage; and when faced with peril and death he was brave enough to stay the course with dignity right to the end. I pray that I should be such a captain one day.*

Mister John Carver, First Mate of the Intrepid

"That's so sad," Amanda said in a soft voice. My thoughts exactly as I closed the journal.

"Wait, Peggy, there's one last thing you should read," said Captain Hunter. "I stuck something in that'll interest you."

I flipped to the back of the journal and found a yellowed piece of paper. It was a very old clipping from a newspaper called *The Shipwreck Times*. The headline read: "American Fur Trading Company Loses Ship and Crew." It was dated November 1, 1814 — a year and a half after Mister Carver's final entry.

* * *

The Shipwreck Times is saddened to report that Mister John Astor has lost another of his trading ships in a dispute with the savages of the Northwest. The Intrepid, a fine three-mast barkentine went down on its journey to China. Lost to the world were business partner and gentleman, Mister Robert Lockhart and the distinguished career captain, James Whittaker. All but two of the sixteen crewmen made it back to New York after surviving more than a year amongst the heathen responsible for the tragedy.

Mister Lockhart was murdered while alerting the crew who were fast asleep in their beds. He died a hero. According to Intrepid's First Mate, Mister John Carver, the captain judged it safer to move the ship out to sea in the dark than to stay put until morning. It proved to be the worst possible decision for ship and crew when shortly thereafter a storm arose, forcing them onto the rocks. When it became painfully obvious that the ship and precious cargo was sinking, Captain Whittaker ordered his crew to abandon ship. He himself refused to leave the Intrepid and is now lost to us forever. The surviving men were left to fend for themselves until the arrival of the Voyager a year later. Though they arrived home quite altered they are nonetheless healthy and most certainly grateful to be alive.

"Ironic, isn't it. Even two hundred years ago there were reporters who got the facts wrong," I observed aloud. Everyone laughed. Then I remembered something.

Gina McMurchy-Barber

"Hey, Scott — do you know what a *nian hao* mark is?"

"Sure do ... centuries ago Chinese artisans put their symbols on all pottery or porcelain to show that it was made at the Imperial factory. There were only a small number of highly specialized painters who would have worked for the Chinese emperor. Their styles were so distinct and familiar that we can sometimes identify the artist. Why do you ask?"

"I saw a *nian hao*."

"You did? Where?" he asked, with his brows furrowed.

"Oh, just on the back of that little salt dish that Amanda had me cleaning," I said nonchalantly. I watched his eyes grow big. Then he grinned.

"And how do you know about the Imperial marks?"

"Well, it's a long story that started with my Aunt Margaret's broken china teapot. Let's just say it's one of many mind-numbing facts I miraculously picked up along the way." Everyone laughed.

"Maybe this *leedle* girl is going to be a pottery expert!" said Dr. Sanchez.

"Si, señor. But I don't want to narrow my options — I might want to take up the study of *sheep* worm one day!"

"Don't you mean ship worm?" Amanda said.

"That is what she said — *sheep* worm!" Dr. Sanchez winked at me.

CHAPTER TEN

When I got home I knew I had some changes to make. I'd learned a lot about responsibility and honesty. And I knew that talk was cheap, so if people were going to take me seriously I was going to have to prove to them that I'd learned my lesson. While I made baby steps towards the new me, an article came out in *The Sun* announcing the discovery of the *Intrepid*. It had a photograph of the team — including me. Aunt Margaret was so proud she cut it out to save. Then Mom came home after work with ten more copies.

Captain Hunter — or rather, now that we were land lubbers again, Dr. Hunter — emailed me some photos he took with the underwater camera when we were on our research trip. The best one was of the day I discovered Captain Whittaker's remains. His email read: "We've already received a lot of interest from the B.C. Underwater Archaeology Society and from several organizations across the country. I think we'll be able to get funding for a full-scale excavation of the *Intrepid* within a couple of months. We should also be able to get a remote sensor to help us locate artifacts easier and some new high-tech sonar equipment too. I know you'll be back to school by then, but there's a place for you on the boat if you can arrange to come with us. If you can't, don't worry — this excavation is going to take years." Those words made my heart flutter.

After a day at the beach with TB, I came home and stood looking up to the top of Aunt Margaret's china cabinet where her broken porcelain teapot sat. The glue I'd used had hardened onto the glaze and turned yellow. If I carefully cleaned the surface at least it would look better — even if it would never hold tea again. As gently as I could I brought it down and began to remove the stained glue. That's when Aunt Margaret entered the kitchen. When she saw me holding her precious teapot she looked like she was going to lay an egg.

"What are you doing, Peggy?" she hissed like a wary goose.

"Calm down, Aunt Margaret, I just want to make it look better."

"Don't! Don't try to clean it, or fix it, or anything. Just put it down, please." The look of distress on her face was comical, but I knew better than to laugh. When I put the teapot on the table she exhaled loudly.

"Aunt Margaret, I know a lot more about this old stuff than you think. I'll be careful."

"Old stuff?"

"You know what I mean. Just trust me, please."

"Yes, dear ... trust her." I turned to see Aunt Beatrix standing in the doorway.

"Thanks for the vote of confidence, Aunt Bea." Aunt Margaret frowned — what could she say when even Aunt Beatrix was on my side?

"What was in the large brown envelope that arrived yesterday, dear?" asked Aunt Bea.

"It's my membership papers to the Nautical Archaeology Society. Dr. Hunter recommended me for membership." If I were a light bulb I would have been beaming.

"Well — you see, when you take care of the small things, when you are conscientious, honest, temperate, and polite things go much better."

"That's right, Aunt Bea, it's a person's moment-by-moment conduct that determines the success of her life." My great aunt smiled and nodded her double chins at me. Then she used her nose to point to the closet.

"Oh, right! Aunt Margaret, I have a surprise for you."

"A surprise? I hope it's a nice surprise." She watched me suspiciously while I went to the closet and pulled out a small box.

"Here … I hope you like it," I said as I handed it to her. "It's something Aunt Bea helped me pick out at the Thrift Store — paid for it with my own money too."

"It's not something that's going to jump out at me, is it?"

"No gag, Aunt Margaret. Honest. Go ahead — but be careful, it's fragile." She still looked at me suspiciously, but tenderly removed the object from the box and unwrapped the miles of old newspaper.

"A teapot! It's lovely, Peggy," she beamed. "Thank you." She set it on the kitchen table next to her good one and turned it about to admire the details.

"I'm glad you like it. I know it will never be the same, but at least now you'll have something nice to serve tea in when Aunt Beatrix comes for visits. Right, Aunt Bea?"

"Quite right, dear." Aunt Bea looked at her watch. "Now about that trip to Heron Park you promised me … we haven't got all day you know." I could tell Aunt Margaret was watching to see what I would do. I knew she expected me to make an excuse to get out of it.

"Sure, Aunt Bea, I'm ready if you are." I smiled.

"Well, clearly my child you are not ready …" complained Aunt Bea. Aunt Margaret smirked happily at me.

"What?" I asked. She pointed to my tangled hair and hockey jersey with disgust.

"Okay," I said lightly. "It's too bad though — by the time I've changed my shirt and brushed my hair we won't have time to visit Mr. Grimbal — his store closes shortly."

"Oh, is that so? Well, in that case chop chop — let's go." Aunt Beatrix quickly pulled on her coat and shoved me towards the door. Aunt Margaret opened her mouth to speak but Aunt Beatrix cut her off. "Sorry Margaret, dear … can't talk now." As I turned back, Aunt Margaret was clutching her new teapot and shaking her head.

"Peggy, you'll never cease to surprise me!" Then she threw back her head and laughed … well, it was more like a snort, but nobody noticed except me.

AUTHOR'S NOTE

There were two Pacific fur trading ships that inspired this story. The first was the *Boston* and was commanded by Captain John Salter. He was the kind of man that I modelled Captain Whittaker after. The *Boston* arrived in the Nootka Sound, on Vancouver Island, B.C. in 1803. During trading negotiations there was a dispute between the captain and Chief Maquinna and each man was deeply offended by the other. In retaliation, the Nuu-chah-nulth warriors attacked the crew and sank the ship. There were only two survivors: the blacksmith and the sailmaker. The blacksmith, John Jewitt, survived because Chief Maquinna wanted him to teach his people about blacksmithing. The sailmaker survived because Jewitt said the man was his father — which he was not. The two were held captive by Maquinna for several years. Eventually they were released and Jewitt wrote a book about his experience called *The Adventures and Sufferings of John R. Jewitt*. It's a fascinating book that contains a great deal of ethnographic (cultural) material.

The second ship that was of interest to me in the writing of this book was the *Tonquin*. Unlike Captain Salter, Lieutenant Thorn was a short tempered and ill-mannered American naval officer. Throughout the voyage he showed that he was not a man to be trifled with. On more than one occasion he abandoned crew who did not make their way back to the ship on time. He nearly let his men freeze to death during the voyage north in the cold months; he allowed several to drown in a poorly executed plan to find the passage up the uncharted Columbia River; and he frequently threatened to kill anyone on board who crossed him. In the end it was his disdain and insulting behaviour towards one of the Nuu-chah-nulth chiefs of Clayoquot Sound (on the west coast of Vancouver Island, B.C.) that brought retaliation. After the Nuu-chah-nulth warriors killed the captain and most of the crew, they returned to the ship the next day to claim their prize. But there was a single fatally injured crewman left on board and on June 14, 1811, when he saw the enemy coming, he lit the 9000 pounds of gunpowder aboard and blew up the ship and nearly two hundred warriors. The only survivor of the crew was a half Chinook interpreter. He remained with the Nuu-chah-nulth for a couple of years and then escaped to the south.

Both ships were owned by John Jacob Astor, one of the richest men in the world of that time. When the War of 1812 broke out the British navy frequently captured American trading ships. To avoid losing his ships during the war Astor decided to sell the American Fur Company to British interests in 1813. By this time the sea otter fur trade was beginning to decline, along with the number of otters. To this day the animal is still on the endangered animal list.